GDWOODSBOOKS

PRESENTS

for subscribers to www.gdwoodsbooks.com

w   **Date: 10/17/17**

D1527639

FIC WOODS
Woods, Genevieve D.
Love again /

A GDWOODSBOOKS PUBLICATION

Love Again by **Genevieve D. Woods**
First Edition: February 2017

Copyright © 2017 Genevieve D. Woods

HTTPS://WWW.FACEBOOK.COM/GROUPS/GDWOODSBOOKS/

This book is a work of fiction. The names, characters, and incidents are products of the writer's imagination or have been used fictitiously. Some places are real but they are not actual event unless cited. Otherwise, any resemblance to persons, living or dead, actual events, locales or organizations is entirely coincidental.

About Genevieve

Genevieve D. Woods was born in the South and considers herself a true Southern girl. She is an avid reader of all genres and has a great love of music, which, if you pay close attention, you'll see come through in her writing.

Genevieve is the bestselling author of the Greatest Love Series. *All I'll Ever Ask, After Church, Dawn and Autumn, Just Be Held,* and *The Conclusion* consistently hold steady in the top 50 books in African American Christian Fiction on Amazon.com with *Just Be Held* debuting at #2. With the release of the fifth book, Genevieve's Greatest Love Series reached its conclusion; however, she will be following some of your (and her) favorite characters as they move forward in their lives.

In September 2016, Genevieve released the first of several mini-series that have become a part of her free web series posted on her website and GDWOODSBOOKS Club via Facebook. These stories have been such a hit that she's collected the first set of mini-stories, *It Won't Prosper: A Parable on Infidelity in Marriage*, into a novella, available as an e-book and in print, which was edited from its original web posts and includes bonus material not available anywhere else. GDWOODSBOOKS Club is Genevieve's growing book club that meets monthly, virtually on Facebook and in person. The goal of Genevieve's book club is to give back to the community and support other authors. To learn more about

GDWOODSBOOKS go to
https://www.facebook.com/groups/gdwoodsbooks/.

In regards to her characters, Genevieve writes flawed characters that do not always start out on the right path—they fall down, they curse, they have physical and verbal altercations, they do not deny their flesh. But through the suffering of their Heavenly Father, they find redemption and happiness (in most cases). Genevieve doesn't always agree with her character's actions, but she allows them to follow their paths.

Genevieve lives in Memphis, TN with her husband, three children, and a Shi-Tzu that thinks he's one of the kids. She attributes her success in writing to Christ first, but also the unwavering support of her husband. She describes him as "a solid rock, my muse, the second lover of my soul, and the only lover of my body. I adore him."

You can find Genevieve at www.gdwoodsbooks.com, Amazon, Facebook, Google+.

Acknowledgments

Before you read, I would like first to say thank you for purchasing, *Love Again.* Your purchase/download makes my dreams a reality.

To the Lord of my life, Jesus Christ, thank you for your spirit, mercy, and grace. Without you, I could do nothing. Your praises will forever be on my lips, and it's my desire to give your name the glory with every story that I write.

To my husband of twenty years, thank you for loving me like no other can. You are the inspiration for the Alpha males that I write, who love their ladies like Christ's love for his bride.

To the GDWOODSREADERS Facebook group, thank you for your daily inspiration and allowing me to practice my craft with you. With every episode I write, I eagerly wait for your comments. Each one of you inspires me to Write One.

A special shout out of love goes to; Vickie Merrit, Deborah Dunson, Jacqueline Land, Tosha Andrews, Tina V. Young, Lee Jones, Alicia Lane, Yvette Roberson, Phyllis Miller, Diamond Presswood, Dee Day (deebraidartist), Tommie Davis, Tammy Jernigan, Cortrina Henderson, Carlene Woods, Leah Woods, Brenda Bowen, La Ronda Davis, Shay Grayson, Kimberly Berry-White, Melissa Saulsberry-Smith, Lakisha Johnson, LaQuisha Fields-Rucker, Albertina Herron, Tawanda Andrews, Ki Witherspoon, LaShawn Vasser, Kalee M., Renisa Hoskins, Barbara Ward, Bridgette Brounson, Latasha Wiggins, Lisa Abston, Latonya Broome and Tosha Harris. Without you,

Love Again would not be possible. Thank you for your fellowship online and in person. I look forward to our meetings and your comments in our Facebook group. You keep me motivated.

To my editor, Melissa S. Harrison, thank you for all your efforts in making each book better than the one before. Your reader's comments mean the world to me. Thanks for being part of the GDWOODSBOOKS' team.

To JB Logic Covers, you are truly gifted from above. Thank you for the awesome covers that you deliver each and every time. I am always blown away by what you create for me, and the other authors you design for. Thanks for being part of the GDWOODSBOOKS' team.

To Simply Blessed Promotions, Andrea (Tootie Williams), thank you for the excellence in marketing the GDWOODSBOOKS' brand. You Rock!

To each reader, thanks for giving me a chance, and I hope you enjoy *Love Again*.

A word from the author

Hi,

Before you begin, I wanted to share that this story is a tribute to breast cancer awareness. It is dedicated to everyone who is fighting the battle, won the battle, and in memory of those who have lost the fight to breast cancer. I salute all organizations that help families in need while their loved ones face the battle of a lifetime.

This disease is beatable if detected early. Therefore, I implore you to do self-checks and have annual mammograms. They really do save lives.

As I stated earlier, I began writing this story as a web series for the GDWOODSBOOKS Readers. It was titled, *Lost Pearl*, but as Pastor Titus went through his journey, I renamed it, *Love Again*. It is my prayer that you, the reader, can embrace the fact that sometimes life throws us blows and lands us in great despair. However, all things work together for the good to those who love the Lord and are called according to his purpose. So, it is our duty to get up and to continue the good fight of faith. We don't have the right to give up! We don't have the right to give in!

I praise the following brave women whose lives and families have been affected or taken by breast cancer.

Lillie Mae Phillips

Angela Gillespie – Pegues

Reola Hathaway

Lynette Williams

Act·One

Episode One

Pastor Titus-Timothy Smith entered the hospital room where his wife of twelve years, Pearl, lay peacefully still. He left the pulpit before delivering his sermon after receiving a call from her personal nurse, Lillie, who repeated what the doctors had said, "it was time."

As he made his way into the room, he ignored the spirit of death that was vexing him to his heart. Titus nodded his head, greeting the hospital's nurse who was changing the IV bags. Lillie was standing near the exit of the room; Titus gave her a brief but enduring hug. She walked briskly from the room with tears streaming down her face.

When he reached his loves' bedside, he took her delicate hand from underneath the cover and kissed the back of it, just as he had greeted her since their first day. Titus then moved to her pale forehead and gave her a lingering kiss that matched the longing of his soul. *Why can't she be healed and stay?* He felt the slightest squeeze to his hand and let his gaze travel down. He realized Pearl's eyes were slightly open, and she gave him a small smile and rested them again. If he were not in tune with her, he would have missed that beautiful fleeting moment.

Titus sat down in the hospital chair just as the nurse was leaving the room. He looked around at all the beautiful flowers, fruit baskets, balloons, and cards sent by the congregation and family. They were expressions of love but also served as the celebration of a life ending, which was soul-shattering to him. His consolation was that Pearl had fought the good fight of faith, against breast cancer.

Knowing that he needed strength from the Father above, he reached into his suit jacket and pulled out the sterling silver necklace with the crucifixion cross his mother, Eunice, had given to him when he accepted Christ as a teenager. He always petitioned the Father with it in his hand and while he delivered sermons to God's people. He closed his eyes. He bowed his head . . . and he prayed.

Episode Two

Titus prayed for strength to endure what was about to manifest in his life. As he prayed, visions of Pearl, the day that they met, played vividly in his mind. He was at The City Hospital visiting the members of his church that were hospitalized. He was an Associate Pastor at the time and visiting the sick and shut-in was part of his job responsibility. She was the charge nurse on the senior citizen wing of the hospital. When she looked up from her computer screen, her hazel eyes mesmerized him, and he couldn't remember the brother's name he was there to see. He turned into a mumbling third grader who stuttered. Gone was the man of distinction and cloth, who held a master's degree in Theology and a doctorate in Psychology. He could not even remember his own name. His throat constricted, and his face burned hot. He could not gather his emotions but knew he needed to.

"Sir, are you okay? Do you need to be seen in the emergency room?" Titus could do nothing but pat his chest with his hand, trying to break up whatever was lodged in his throat. He had never felt so flushed in his life.

"Water." He finally uttered. The beauty dashed to the water fountain across from her station and filled a paper cup that she pulled from the dispenser and gave it to him.

"Are you okay, sir?" She asked as she gently rubbed him on the back. Her touch was electrifying. He needed to get away from this lady before he passed out. He was so embarrassed as he noticed he had an audience. The nurse must have noticed and led him to a nearby waiting room. Titus drank the water and managed to pull his church identification badge out of his suit coat. The nurse took it and passed it back.

"So, you are a Pastor, are you here to see someone?" He nodded his head in the affirmative.

"Well, I am nurse Pearl Matthews. When you are ready, just let me know who you need to see, and I will escort you." She rose from her seat next to him and made her way back to her station. Inwardly, Pearl had butterflies in her stomach. When she touched his back, out of concern, she felt electricity like never before. She had no doubt that Pastor Titus Timothy would be in her life.

Titus gave himself a few minutes to collect his emotions. This had been the most embarrassing day of his life, but he was there to do a job. He approached Nurse Matthews and asked for Peter Robinson's room, and Nurse Matthews escorted him to the room. After he had finished praying with Brother Robinson and spending quality time with him, Titus asked Nurse Pearl out for coffee. When she said yes was when his breathing returned to normal. After their first date, he knew she was the one.

Episode Three

Time seemed to speed by during the months Titus and Pearl dated. They found out they loved many of the same things, amusement parks, biking, long walks on the riverfront watching the sunset by the Mississippi River. Most importantly, they shared the same belief in the Lord. Pearl began attending his church, and she became a member after he was promoted to Pastor. Their lives seemed just to fall into place and, along with all the other positives, their families adored them both. Therefore, after one year of dating, while they were attending a Redbirds game at the AutoZone Park, Pearl looked up on the Jumbotron and gasped when she saw herself and Titus, kneeling on one knee, with a stadium employee holding the microphone.

"Pearl, you are the most beautiful woman I know, inside and out. The first time I met you, I was awestruck by your radiance to the point that I experienced a panic attack trying to form the words to introduce myself. This past year, you have filled my life with joy; you have touched my heart in places I've never known I had. It would make me proud if you joined your life with mine as my wife. Pearl, will you marry me?"

With the biggest smile on her face, Pearl screamed, "Yes!"

They kissed, and the jumbotron went to the kissing cam. Pearl spent the rest of the game staring adoringly between her three-karat diamond engagement ring and her husband to be.

One year later, they were married by the Bishop of their denomination before thousands of guests. They honeymooned in Jamaica where Titus took his bride for the first time. They were hopeful about their new beginning in life and ministry.

Episode Four

The first few years of marriage were full of bliss. Titus and Pearl were one in every way. Pearl resigned from the hospital and went full-time in the ministry. She developed a Healthcare Ministry for the saints of their church and the surrounding community. Titus' love for God and his people grew their congregation from eight hundred members to eight thousand. They were truly blessed.

The first test of their marriage came at year five when they wanted to add children to their family. For eighteen months, they tried and tried, but every month the pregnancy test was negative. They went to doctor after doctor, and finally, Pearl received a diagnosis of fibroid tumors that were preventing her from becoming pregnant.

The cure was simple; she would have a surgical procedure to remove the tumors, and they could begin their family. But, that was not in the will of God. During the surgery, they discovered the tumors had caused irrevocable damage to Pearl's uterus, and a full hysterectomy was performed. That was a dark day for them when Pearl woke up after surgery and was informed by her husband that children weren't possible. She went into a deep depression.

Titus was there by her side, praying for her, loving her, until she came out of the depths of despair. He attended counseling with her, and after a year, Pearl accepted she would not be anyone's biological mother. She didn't want to go through the adoption process. Instead, Pearl revamped the Nursery and Children's Ministry, and that was enough for them both.

The last few years were spent doing the Lord's work and traveling the world on romantic getaways. They had gone to Dubai, Milan, Egypt, The Virgin Islands, Australia, Japan, and nearly every state in America.

Episode Five

~Pearl Matthews Smith, age 39, Memphis, TN~
On January 14, 2016, the Lord wrapped his arms around Pearl, his angel, and called her home to no more pain and suffering after a two-year battle with stage 4 metastatic breast cancer at the City Hospital. Pastor Titus Timothy Smith was at his wife's side singing Amazing Grace as his wife's personal nurse said her goodbyes. Their friends, family, and church congregation waited in the halls and listened as their Pastor said Goodbye to the Pearl that they had all lost.

Act·Two

Episode Six
Ten months later

Titus knelt beside the pearl headstone and ran his fingers down the picture of his beloved wife. Pearl's smile, even on her tombstone, brought warmth to his chilled being. Titus visited his wife daily to be near her. He knew her body had returned to dust, and she was now with the Lord, but there in the cemetery was where he felt comfort. He had purchased the finest headstone with her image to allow her beauty to shine on all that passed by her final resting place. He would read the word of God and bask in the dimming sun of fall.

Today, he opened his Bible to Isaiah chapter six, verse nine. He read the scriptures aloud. "And he said, 'Go, and tell this people, Hear ye indeed, but understand not; and see ye indeed, but perceive not. Make the heart of this people fat, and make their ears heavy, and shut their eyes; lest they see with their eyes, and hear with their ears, and understand with their heart, and convert, and be healed.' "

Titus looked up to heavens, and a quickening happened. He could feel it in his gut, in his very soul. The passage he read was telling him that it was time for him to return to his flock and preach the gospel of Christ. It was time for him to continue the good work of faith.

He lifted his hands in surrender at the foot of Pearl's grave and surrendered his grief to the Lord and accepted His will to live in obedience to the Holy Spirit. He rose, gathered his blanket and study material, smiled at his beautiful Pearl's picture, and decreed within himself losing her would not be in vain. He would honor those that were fighting breast cancer and the memory of those who had lost their battle. He left the cemetery with a renewed spirit; he may have Lost Pearl, but he, Titus Timothy Smith, would live and not die.

Episode Seven

The time Titus took off, the months of bereavement, was now over. He stood in his office, putting on his robe, about to return to the sanctuary for the first time as a widower. Titus looked at the man in the mirror and recognized the weight he had lost while grieving. His robe hung looser than the last time he had worn it. Losing weight shouldn't have been an option with the amount of food the church mothers prepared and sent for him. Not to mention all the single women of various ages that dropped by his home in the name of *checking on him*. He was not interested in any of their subtle or obvious advances. He had lost his Pearl and was going to take the necessary time to mourn. That is what he did, but today was a new day. He had to get back to living; Pearl would want that, this he knew for sure. As he walked into his in-office restroom, his mind went back to a conversation he had with Pearl on one of her last days.

"Babe, I want you to live a full life after I've left this life. I mean it. I want you to marry someone and have children with her." Titus looked at his wife as if she had grown a second head and took her hands in his and kissed the back of them.

"Sweetie, we are not talking about this. I'm still expecting a miracle for you to be healed. I have long since gotten over not being able to have children."

"Titus, you can have kids, I couldn't. Now I see why that was not in the will of God for me. Children would have made me having this disease that much worse if a child were losing me as a mother." Pearl, using the little strength she had, took her hands from Titus and pushed herself into a sitting position. "Titus Timothy Smith, you listen to me good. You will go on after this. You will marry

and have children. You will be the man God has called you to be in the natural and spirit." With that, Pearl leaned her head back on her hospital bed pillows and rested her eyes. She was done with the matter and had accepted her time was near to be with the Lord. It was well with her soul.

"Excuse me, Pastor, are you ready to go into the service?" Titus knew the voice calling out to him was his assistant, Deacon Dewayne Douglas. He finished washing his hands free of his hair products, dried them, and exited the restroom.

"Good Morning, Deacon Dewayne. I am ready."

"Great, we are happy to have you back, Pastor. I have your tablet, necklace, and prayer cloth."

"Then I guess we are ready." The two men made their way out of the pastoral office and started their walk down the hallway that led to the sanctuary.

***

Walking into the sanctuary, Titus could feel the Spirit of the Lord. He looked out at the congregation and saw all the members rise to their feet to honor his arrival. The church was full, and that made his heart glad. The choir was singing, "The Best Day of My Life," by the

Potter's House of Denver. As Titus shook hands with his
ministerial staff on the podium, he took in the lyrics of the
song and received them as confirmation that this was the
new beginning of his life.

> *Today will be/ the best day/ the best day of my life*
>
> *I get my joy back . . .*
>
> *Today I get my heart back . . .*
>
> *Today I get my life back . . .*
>
> *Today for today/ will be the best day/ the*
> *best day of my life*

Titus embraced the words of the song and allowed
the spirit to lead him. He delivered a message entitled,
"Thou shall live and not die." The congregation received it,
and their souls were blessed. Following the service, he
greeted hundreds. Afterward, he agreed to have dinner with
some of the ministers on staff and their wives. They dined
at Southern Hands Family Dining.

"Pastor, now that you are back, what do you see
your focus being?" Associate Minister Thomas asked Titus.

"I'm looking to expand our Health Ministry into a
full clinic with a focus on women's health and breast
cancer awareness and prevention. As a matter of fact, I'm
looking for a professional in that area to bring on the staff,"

Titus said and picked up his utensils to cut into his tender baked chicken and gravy."

"That sounds like a great tribute to First Lady Pearl," replied Thomas.

"Pastor, what qualifications are you looking for in the candidate for the health facility? The reason I ask is, my best friend, Dr. Tosha Hightower, is an oncologist who only works on medical cases as needed by the hospital. She has devoted the majority of her time to her foundation Sister Survivors. I think you may want to interview her." Tina, Deacon Dewayne's wife, said.

"Yes, of course, please give me her information, and I will reach out. Or better yet, Deacon Dewayne, do you mind contacting her and getting her on my calendar as soon as possible?"

"No problem, sir, I will do it first thing in the morning." Deacon Dewayne said and gave his wife a sideways look. She had always commented to him that Tosha would be a perfect match for the pastor. Now here she was setting this up. He chuckled and returned to his baked pork chops. The rest of the dinner was filled with conversation about the next phase of the ministry and small

talk. By the end of the day, Titus was tired but revived. He
honestly felt like today had been the best day of his life.

Episode Eight

Dr. Tosha Hightower could not believe, of all
mornings, she had awakened late this morning. She had an
important meeting with Pastor Smith about his church
becoming a partner with Sister Survivors. Tosha was
frantically scrambling in her downtown condo, getting
dressed and making sure she had all her presentation
material. She was elated yesterday when her friend Tina
had called her and set up the appointment. Her heart went
out to Pastor Smith. She knew he had lost his wife to Breast
Cancer. During her career as an oncologist, she had lost
many patients to cancer. However, through the progression
made from research funded by organizations like Pastor
Smith was the leader of, many lives had been saved. That
was why she was grabbing her cup of coffee from the
Keurig and her briefcase off her island bar, making a mad
dash out of her home. Partnering with Pastor Smith could
be the joint effort that propelled Sister Survivors to the top
as a leading non-profit in Breast Cancer Awareness and
finding a cure.

***

A half hour later, Tosha was being escorted into a large office by Deacon Douglas. She took in the splendor of Pastor Titus' office. It was masculine but had a warm and safe feel to it. It was an odd feeling for Tosha; she rarely felt warmth and safety just by entering a room. She could not ponder on that feeling long. A strikingly handsome man came out of what she assumed was the restroom.

Her heart missed a beat. She had seen Pastor Smith several times before, but it was always in his clergy robe. The man that was walking toward her with his hand outstretched, to greet her in a professional manner, was fashioned of the stuff dreams were made of. Tosha attempted to collect her thoughts and inwardly scolded herself. This man just lost his wife. She needed to get it together. When their hands connected, she felt a bolt of energy go through every limb of her body. She was determined not to show her immediate attraction and slight anxiety as she greeted Pastor Smith.

"Hello, Dr. Hightower, I am so happy you could make it on such short notice. Please have a seat," Pastor Smith said to Tosha.

Tosha saw his mouth moving and heard what had to be his words, but she had no idea what he said. If it weren't for him motioning to the seat across from his large cherry wood desk, she would have been frozen where she stood. She followed his hand like a zombie because she was caught up in his presence. *Lord help me through this meeting.*

Episode Nine

Titus came out of his restroom and was captivated by the sight of, who he assumed was, Dr. Tosha Hightower. She was gorgeous—cocoa skin, beautiful brown eyes with splashes of cinnamon. Dr. Hightower wore a fitted silk gray blouse that gave her a look of elegance and a fitted skirt; the kind Pearl called a pencil skirt. Suddenly, his heart squeezed in his chest. It was the first time he'd had these feelings about anyone other than Pearl. He cleared his throat and stretched out his hand, needing to place a barrier between them. His plan was to greet her with a polite handshake. However, when he held her hand his entire body warmed and parts came alive that hadn't in over a year.

"Good Morning, Dr. Hightower. Thanks for coming on such short notice, please have a sit." After Dr. Hightower was seated, he then turned to the Deacon. "Thank you, Deacon Dewayne, that will be all."

Titus didn't give either of them a chance to respond and scurried to get behind his desk and take a seat. He needed to conceal his body's reaction to this beauty. He had no idea what to make of his instant attraction to the doctor, but he was a man of God and still mourning the loss of his wife. He had to bring his flesh into subjection. He hadn't reacted like this since he met Pearl.

***

Deacon Dewayne turned to exit the office. He was eager to leave these two alone. His meddling wife was right. These two would make a beautiful couple. Tina had been praying and fasting for the pastor and said she felt in her spirit that Dr. Hightower would be perfect for the new Health Ministry and their spiritual leader. Now, after he witnessed their meeting, his wife was right. He shut the door quietly behind him and looked up to the heavens. "Thank you, Lord. Our pastor is going to be all right."

Episode Ten

They were an hour into the meeting, and Titus was impressed by Tosha's intellect and what she had accomplished at such an early age. Their meeting had become business casual shortly after it began. Tosha told him about her college years, medical school, residency, surgical internship, and finally, her working at the city's hospital as an Oncology Surgeon, all before the age of thirty-five. Titus was intrigued by this woman, to say the least.

"You have an impressive list of accomplishments, and the ideas you have presented to begin our Health Ministry with the focus on Breast Cancer for women and Prostate Cancer for men is a direction I would like to go."

Tosha was happy to hear Pastor Smith wanted to proceed with establishing a Health Ministry in his church. A partnership with a ministry like Pastor Smith's was what she had been praying for to gain more supporters for Sister Survivors. The fact that he was interested in their Brother's Keeper chapter was even better.

"That is great, Pastor. What do you need from me to help implement these ministries?"

Titus wanted to say, *remove those perfect dimples on each of your cheeks and those pearly white teeth that*

accentuate and make the thickness of your lips kissable.
But he didn't. Instead, he proposed something he could not believe himself.

"I would like to go over the structure of the Health Ministry over dinner. I understand you, being a medical doctor, have a full schedule. Though, I'm more than willing to work around it."

Tosha eyes widened in surprise to his dinner invitation. She wanted to say let's go now, but she had to remember this meeting was about business. It didn't matter that she could now see herself giving birth to his children. It had been all Tosha could do to hold herself together from weeping as he shared the testimony of the diagnosis and demise of his wife, Pearl. Now, he was pushing forward to honor her memory. Tosha's friend, Tina, had told her he was a special man, but after meeting Pastor Titus, she now knew he was extraordinary.

"My schedule is not as full as you think. I only do consults at the hospital now when needed. My priority is with my charitable organization and gaining supporters for it. I have found that helping patients prevent the disease, provide testing for early detection or pay for their treatment is more rewarding to me and my calling. So, I am free most evenings."

Titus did not miss a beat. "So, we will go to dinner tonight. Please write down your address, and I will pick you up at eight."

Titus pushed a pad and pen toward her. Without a second thought, Tosha wrote down 1670 Park Street and added her personal mobile number.

Act·Three

Episode Eleven

Titus was nervous as he stepped out of his pearl 2016 Mercedes-Benz S-Class. He was dressed in a tailor-made black suit with a black and white pinstriped dress shirt and black silk tie. His black shoes were imported. He walked with a swag that could easily mean he was not just a Godly man but one that could easily grace the cover of GQ magazine. In spite of this, his outer appearance shielded the turmoil that was going on inside of him.

Titus had begun to regret this date. *Because, make no mistake, it was a date.* He and Dr. Hightower could have finished their business in his office, but he wanted to see her on a personal level. He was drawn to her beauty, intelligence, and connected with her in a way that reminded him of his connection with Pearl. That was what gave him pause. *Was it too soon? Was he just lonely? What would his members think? What did the Lord think? What would Jesus do?* By the time he pushed the doorbell, Titus was beginning to perspire from all the anxiety raging inside.

When Dr. Tosha Hightower opened the door, wearing a fitted black dress and looking beautiful, the anxiety he was experiencing all but vanished. He stepped back so she could exit her front door. When she turned to lock and secure her home, he took her in from behind and liked what he saw. As she made her way toward him, he proffered his hand, and she took it, rewarding him with a beautiful smile. He knew there was something between him and this woman.

"Good Evening, Tosha. You look amazing."

"Thank you," she responded, causing her dimples to deepen.

"You are handsome as well, Titus. I look forward to tonight." They made their way to the car. Titus opened the passenger door for her and then personally buckled her in. It wasn't lost on either of them that all professional pretenses had been tossed to the side. They were on an official first date.

Titus took her to the Tower Room American Grill located on the thirty-third floor of the Clark Tower building. The restaurant offered a fantastic view of the city. One could see the Mississippi River Bridge, and the *M* sparkled through the windows as they had their meal. Their conversation began with starting up the Pearl Health Ministry. By dessert, they had laughed about the past, and Tosha had shed tears as Titus shared his memories about his life with Pearl. The fact that she was genuinely moved by his testimony of love lost had secured her place in his heart. Tosha had never been a woman who was looking for a man. She had an amazing career and a life mission to help the afflicted. She was also a woman full of the Holy Spirit, and she knew when Titus was walking her back to her front door and kissed her sweetly on the cheeks that He. Was. The. One.

Episode Twelve

As the weeks passed, Dr. Tosha Hightower was doing a superb job implementing the new Pearl Health Ministry at Kingdom Building Ministries (KBM). The board of trustees and the deacons were happy with the new outreach. So much so, they approved an additional health wing to be added to the church. Titus was overjoyed with happiness because he could honor Pearl's memory. He felt like she was shining down on his budding relationship with Tosha. He never thought for a moment that he could feel passion for someone other than Pearl, but in so many ways, Tosha felt like an extension of Pearl. He knew that was an odd thought and would never verbally say it to anyone, but in his heart, his relationship with Tosha felt right. She was attending as many services as she could. They were not always on Sunday because those days she sat with patients who were in chemo treatment. His thoughts went back to a date where the two of them discussed what ministry was. It was over an early dinner at Houston's Restaurant.

"Tosha, I'm pleased that you agreed to be on staff officially, and you attending Bible study and services makes me so happy." Titus loved to watch Tosha smile. Her dimples deepened when she smiled, and it was like sunshine shining through the clouds on a dim day.

"I love attending and hearing you expound on the word. I thought you wouldn't be happy I didn't attend on more Sunday mornings." Tosha picked up her glass of water.

"No, I understand what you are doing is ministry. It is selfless of you to sit with chemo patients and nurse them back to health. That is doing the Lord's work, Tosha. Attending church on Sunday is to refuel the Saints for service. However, ministry is outside of those church walls. I never want you to stop that, ever." Titus picked up Tosha's left hand and kissed the palm of it. She was beginning to mean so much to him.

Titus came out of his thoughts with a smile on his face just as he heard a knock on his office door.

"Come in."

Sister Barbara Stoneheart, a woman who felt she should be the next Mrs. Titus Smith, walked in. She had known him since they were in the children's choir, and she had been working at KBM as the Executive Administrative Assistant for the last several years. When Sister Pearl took ill, she was right by her side. She helped by doing whatever the first couple of the church needed. When Pearl passed, she made sure the funeral arrangements were on point and Repast was a feast to behold, all because of her. While the Pastor grieved, she made sure breakfast, lunch, and dinner were served daily to his home. These things she did out of the kindness of heart because she knew the Lord would repay her for her works. She expected that payment to come in the form of her name being changed from Barbara Stoneheart to Barbara Smith. However, all she got was a plaque and a thank you upon his return, but she was a patient woman. She had thought that he might have needed more time to heal—Pearl was a phenomenal woman. But, with the little doctor always at his side, she could see he had healed just fine.

Barbara was entering the Pastor's office with a chip on her shoulder. He and his board may have thought things were going well with this new addition to the staff and his personal life, but Barbara and her crew felt different. She was becoming the joke of the women's ministry. All the ladies knew she was after a ring from the Pastor.

Unfortunately, he did not give her the time of day, and everyone knew it. Barbara could take no more of his insults after seeing a spacious new office with a gold-plated nameplate on the door that said, *Dr. Tosha Hightower, Director of Pearl Health Ministry.* It was time for somebody to say something, and she was just the person for the job.

Episode Thirteen

Astounded, Titus sat as his long-term friend and administrative assistant listed her complaints. He had not seen this coming. He always viewed Barbara as a friend. They had grown up together in this very church. Sure, she was a beautiful, good-figured woman, but their relationship had transitioned from friends to boss and subordinate when he took the role as lead pastor. When Pearl began attending Kingdom Building Ministries, Barbara was the first person he introduced Pearl to, and the two of them became the best of friends. There was no way he could ever view Barbara as anything other than a friend and dedicated employee to the ministry. But being the patient man he was, Titus listened.

Barbara adjusted herself in her seat as she spoke to Titus. His expression was always hard to read, but she laid her heart on the table all the same.

"Pastor Titus, I just don't think it is fair how you brought in Dr. Hightower and thrust her on us. She does not know the KBM way, nor did she know my best friend, Pearl. Who, by the way, has not been dead in the ground a solid year yet." Barbara paused, regretting the last statement. She looked for Titus to rebuke her, but he said nothing.

"I'm just saying that there are health professionals already here that would have liked and deserved a chance at leading Pearl's Health Ministry. Then there is a host of woman who care about your well-being on a personal level, including me. I want to see you happy and not taken advantage of. That is why for months, I came to your house, prepared meals, and cleaned while you grieved. You deserve a woman that can be that to you. Can this doctor?"

Barbara stopped again to gauge Titus' temperature or to give him a chance to respond. Before he could, there was a knock on his door, which prompted Titus to speak.

"Come in." To Titus' delight and Barbara's horror, Dr. Tosha entered the office. Titus rose to his feet. Even though Barbara could never read his expression, she could read it now. Pastor Titus had a look of love across his beautiful, chiseled face, and Barbara's heart broke. She watched as Titus strolled over and gathered Tosha in an embrace and placed a kiss on her cheek. He escorted her hand in hand over to meet Barbara.

"Sis Barbara, I would like you to formally meet the Director of Pearl's Health Ministry and my lady, Dr. Tosha Hightower." Barbara felt the sting of his words within her depths, but she was determined to hold it together. She stood up, straightened her skirt and blouse, then greeted Dr. Tosha with a handshake.

"Sweetheart, Sister Barbara has been a friend of mine since we sang in the children's choir. She was also dear to Pearl and is a great asset to our ministry. She was expressing her desire to extend support to you because she knows how much this ministry means to me and the memory of Pearl." Tosha was excited to hear the news. She was wondering when she would start to get department helpers. She smiled her beautiful dimpled smile that melted Titus's heart but made Barbara hot.

"Sister Barbara, I would love to go over the plans for the ministry with you and have you show me the ropes."

What could Barbara do? Titus had put her in her place. She had to follow along.

"Of course, just come up to the administration floor when you are ready to start." Barbara picked up her purse, but before leaving, she turned to Titus.

"Pastor, are you going to give any thought to or answer my concerns?"

"Sister Barbara, I have and trust that I only want the best for the ministry and all its members. Thanks for coming to me. My door is always open."

"Thank you for your time, Pastor."

Outside of the office, Barbara was fuming, but what else could she do? She couldn't report to the other ladies that she had failed. There had to be another way to stop this train wreck.

Episode Fourteen

Behind his closed door, Titus took in the full pleasure of Tosha's presence. They were still standing and holding hands.

"You look beautiful today," he said to Tosha as he led her to the seat Barbara had vacated.

"Thanks, and you are handsome today as usual." Tosha gave him her dazzling smile as he took his seat behind his desk.

"So, Dr. Hightower, what have you been up to today?"

"I visited the hospital where I checked on some of my chemo patients, met with a potential donor for Sister Survivors, and had lunch with Tina before I came here. What about you? How has your day been?"

Titus rubbed his head and then stroked his chin, trying to decide on how to answer her question. "It began as a usual day with budget meetings. I participated in the early morning prayer hour with the missionaries and then came back to my office to do paperwork." He hesitated before continuing. Although they had been dating just a few months, Tosha already knew his signals of distress. She leaned in to lock eyes with him.

"What happened to make today take an unusual turn of events?" Tosha had an idea it was related to Sister Barbara. The lady came off polite enough, but there was something in her eyes that said beware. Tosha wanted Titus to open up to her about his troubles, and she would be there to listen and support him. But she was not going to drag it out of him. She waited patiently for Titus to answer her. After several seconds that seemed like several hours to Tosha, he spoke.

"Sister Barbara came into my office to voice her complaints about your position with the Pearl Health Ministry and the role you have in my personal life." Tosha sat back in her chair with a frown on her face.

"Sister Barbara, the lady you just offered to be on my staff, has issues with me professionally and personally? And you think it's a good idea for her to work with me?" Tosha raised an eyebrow and folded her arms across her chest.

"Yes. I did that so she can get to know you and understand why you are my choice for the ministry and my life." Titus stood up as he was speaking and took the chair next to Tosha. He took both of her soft, manicured hands into his. "Tosha, that is what you are—my choice professionally and personally. I want you to feel secure in that truth. You are not just a fill in for Pearl or a haphazard choice. I have fallen in love with you and see a lifetime of happiness in our future."

Tosha was happy to hear these words, but it still didn't make sense to her why he was throwing her to the wolves with this Sister Barbara lady. Titus could see the confusion in her eyes and addressed what he felt was causing it.

"I introduced you to Barbara the way I did to let her know you are my choice, and she, and any of the other ladies that thought they were doing groundwork while I was in mourning, by cooking and cleaning for me, would be getting *only* gratitude for their service." He paused. "As my lady and a senior member of my staff, Tosha, you must work professionally with these women. They are a part of KBM. Do you think you can handle it?" Tosha held Titus' hands and considered his eyes, thinking about Titus' question. She felt like there was more to it than, "could she get along with others?"

To himself, Titus was praying that Tosha understood that some women were faithful to the church because they wanted a chance to be the next first lady. To some, it had nothing to do with him, but the power of that title. He hated that Barbara, whom he thought was a friend to him and his late wife, showed him differently today. But he couldn't throw her out of the church, and Tosha was going to have to deal with quite a few more Barbaras.

"I understand what you are saying, Titus, but that doesn't mean I want them on my staff. They have already been giving me evil stare downs. But I will not approve of anyone who already has something against me to be on my department's roster. That is a professional deal breaker for me." Tosha removed her hands from Titus, folded them together in her lap, and gave Titus what he could only describe as a "what now?" look. He smiled at Tosha, causing the wall she had erected to come tumbling down.

"Fair enough, Dr. Hightower. How about this? We will place an ad on LinkedIn and in the church's job bulletin. You can interview the applicants and build your staff with those you are comfortable with." Titus stood, leaned over, and kissed her sweetly on the forehead. He then whispered in her ear, "I'm proud of you for standing your ground with me. I would have been disappointed if you had let that slide." Tosha looked up at Titus with a look of incredulity.

"Was that a test?"

"No. It is the reality that you will live as my lady and for entering this ministry as the head of a department. Church people think there is an understood seniority line, which only exists in their clicks. I need you strong and not to fall victim to these types of people. It is disheartening to me that Pearl's best friend is now one of those people."

"So, it was a test, and I passed, right?" Tosha said with glee in her voice. Titus held his stern demeanor.

"It was not a test, but you have proved that you are more than capable of this journey with me." With that, he smiled and gave her a wink. Tosha burst into laughter and got up.

"Let me get to work, Pastor." She picked up her purse, placed a hand on his desk, and leaned over giving him a kiss on the cheek.

"Dinner at my house tonight?" Titus asked as he accepted her kiss.

"Sure, I will pick it up and be over by six." With that, Tosha left, closing the door behind her, leaving Titus feeling like a man walking on air.

Tosha felt like she was on a cloud as she leaned back on his closed office door. The man of her dreams had just told her she was not a fill-in but his future.

Episode Fifteen

Tosha was putting on the last of her makeup when she heard her doorbell ring. It was member appreciation Sunday at KBM, and Titus asked her to be his personal guest. Tosha had been attending KBM since she had become a member of staff and started dating Titus; however, this would be the first Sunday she would arrive with him. It felt like he was making a statement to the congregation. Lord knew the women of KBM had been making statements to Tosha, especially when she declined to hire Barbara Stoneheart onto her staff. If it weren't for her friend Tina Douglas, she wouldn't have a friend there at all. But she was not going to let that deter her from her role at KBM or make her regret being the lady in Titus's life. With one final pucker of her lips, she grabbed her clutch purse, turned off her bedroom light, and made her way to greet her man.

When Tosha opened her front door, Titus' knees almost buckled. She was beautiful. But he was no weakling. He manned up and reached for her hand, kissing her palm.

"Good Morning, Dr. Hightower." He always greeted her formally on their initial encounter, something Tosha adored.

"Good Morning, Pastor Smith." Titus lifted his head as he released Tosha's hand and took in her beautiful black lace dress. He noticed how she accessorized it with pure white pearl earrings, necklace, and bracelet. She was just marvelous.

Tosha set the security code to her front door and allowed her handsome date slash pastor to escort her to his Mercedes. She wasn't sure why he needed to pick her up, but she was happy he seemed *all in* regarding their relationship. As they drove, her mind went back to a few days ago, when Barbara Stoneheart tried to plant seeds of doubt into her heart and mind.

Tosha was going over resumes for potential candidates for the Pearl Health Ministry Staff when there was a knock at her door. Without glancing up, she said, "Come in."

When the door opened, Tosha heard a female voice say, "Is this a good time?" She looked up to find Sister Barbara Stoneheart. Without hesitation, Tosha stood and said, "Come in Sister Barbara and have a seat." Barbara took a chair flanking Tosha's desk.

"How may I help you this afternoon?"

Barbara tried to put on her nicest possible voice.

"I was wondering if you had a chance to review my resume and if you will be calling me to be a part of the Pearl Health Ministry staff?" Tosha was surprised. She thought Titus was going to handle this with Barbara. Apparently, she thought wrong.

"Yes, I did review your resume. Right now, you are not one of the candidates I have selected to interview for my staff." All niceties were gone where Barbara was concerned. This woman had already gone to Titus to complain about her, and Tosha had a sneaking suspicion that Barbara had feelings for him. Barbara leaned over the desk with her hand on her hip.

"What do you mean I won't be interviewed for your staff? This Health Ministry is in memoriam of my best friend. You won't find anybody more suited to carry this

ministry forward as Pearl would have wanted than I would."

"That may be true, Sister Barbara. You may be able to perform a ministry as First Lady Pearl would have deemed appropriate; however, this department is only named in memory of her. The day to day functions will follow the health requirements mandated by the state of Tennessee." Tosha raised an eyebrow at Barbara to see if she was following. "Do you understand, Sister Barbara?"

"What do you mean, do I understand? I may not have all those fancy degrees like you, but I am not dumb. You know, you've got another thing coming if you think you are going to push out the good people of Kingdom Building Ministries to suit your agenda and bring people off the street that doesn't know a thing about KBM or First Lady Pearl." Barbara stood up. Before she began to walk away, she had one more thing to add. She leaned over Tosha's desk, invading her personal space. "You need to get any thought out of that brilliant, conniving little head of yours of you becoming the next Mrs. Titus Timothy Smith. It. Isn't. Gonna. Happen." With that, Barbara stormed out of Tosha's office and slammed the door.

Tosha came out of her reverie. She hadn't addressed the Barbara situation with Titus yet but planned on it.

Before she knew it, they were pulling onto the church grounds. Titus parked in the pastor's garage and got out of the car. He made his way around to open the door for Tosha. When they entered his office, Deacon and Sister Douglas were waiting on them. They had morning prayer together for the anointing of the service. This was something that the couple did with the Pastor and First Lady Pearl. Titus had asked Sister Tina to begin the prayer this morning with Tosha. The Douglases were happy to do so as they felt the couple was ordained by God. After the prayer, Titus asked if he could have a moment with Tosha.

Tosha had no idea what was going on or why Tina had been standing guard with her husband, Dewayne, like she was waiting to assist her personally. Confused, she watched them walk out and shut the door behind them. She turned to ask Titus what was going on, but he was on bended knee with an open ring box in his hand.

Episode Sixteen

Before Tosha could utter a word, Titus was speaking.

"Tosha, when I *lost Pearl*, I thought I would never find the strength to breathe again, least of all, *love again*. But God touched my heart and soul, filling it with the courage to go on. I stopped worrying about all the missed opportunities I had lost and began to worship Him and hear what His will was for me. That is when Tina recommended you to start the Health Ministry to honor Pearl and to help those who are physically in need. I never imagined she would be introducing me to the missing piece of my heart, my life, my being. That is what you are to me, Tosha Dunson Hightower; you are the gem that makes my life and ministry whole. Will you take this ring and agree to be my forever—in love—physically, spiritually—and in matrimony and ministry?"

Titus looked up at his beautiful, misty-eyed lady and prayed a *yes* was soon to come. She was still as a statue with one hand covering her mouth as if she was in shock. He said a silent prayer, *Lord, please let her say yes. I'm down here on my knees.* When Tosha remained silent, he cleared his throat. "Sweetheart, I need—an-uh answer."

Tosha came out of her shock and screamed, "Yes, I will marry you!"

Titus got up and put the ring on her finger and spun her around. Once he put her back on her feet and began to wipe the tears from her eyes, he said, "You had me worried for a second there."

Tosha was smiling through the tears that Titus couldn't keep up with and responded, "I'm sorry, Titus, I love you so much. There wasn't any doubt. It's just . . . when you know you want to become a doctor, you must stay focused and realize that dating, love, and perhaps a family, may not happen. I believed for the longest time that I could not have it all. Now I'm standing here with the career that I love, with the man I love, soon to be a wife, and hopefully a mother." She fell onto Titus' muscular chest and cried tears of joy.

Their timing perfect, Deacon Dewayne and Sister Tina knocked then entered the Pastor's office with caution. Pastor Titus smiled at them as he held his fiancée and caressed her back. The Douglases' smiles were from ear to ear. Sister Tina elbowed Dewayne in the side and said, "Told you so."

When Tosha had collected herself, the Douglases gave the couple their congratulations. Tina and Tosha fawned over the five-carat engagement ring. Before they could get carried away in their bliss, Pastor Titus had to call order for the day.

"Sweetheart, I am beyond blessed that you have accepted my proposal. I'm sure you know by now that this was planned with the Douglases' help." Tosha nodded yes while smiling and twisting her new ring.

"Because you are now the future first lady of KBM, Sister Tina will be your assistant as the lady-elect. She will be with you at any social functions or classes that are outside the Health Ministry. She will sit with you during the service and at the member appreciation dinner. She and Deacon Douglas will sit at our assigned table."

Titus' heart dropped as he saw Tosha's smile fade away. But he had to quickly make her see the ugly side of the church world.

"Honey, I know you may be wondering why, just trust me. I will announce you as my fiancée today, and some people won't like it."

Tosha interrupted him. "You mean some women?"

Titus hunched his shoulders up not wanting to debate. "Yes, some women will not like it, but Sister Tina will be by your side to help you through this, okay?"

Tosha was once again stunned, but she was not about to let the devil or any woman steal her joy. She looked to Tina and said, "Good thing we are besties, right?"

Tina gave her a hug and said, "I got you, girl." The ladies were about to exit when Titus called out.

"I need a moment with my fiancée if you all don't mind."

"Of course, not." Tina and Dewayne said in unison and left out of the office leaving the two lovebirds alone. Tosha turned and walked toward Titus as he met her in the middle of the room. He took her by her left hand and kissed it gently, and then placed a kiss on her lips. Taking a step back, he just looked at her, admiring her beauty that radiated from inside out. Tosha stood there captivated by him as well, filled with hope of what the future held for them.

"Thank you for saying yes, babe. I love you and will care for you and treat you the way you deserve—always.

Tosha, left speechless by the moment, closed the space between them and put her hands around his neck. He bent down, making it easier for her to whisper in his ear.

"Titus, it is with joy that I agreed to be yours. I will love you until my last breath." Titus grabbed Tosha by the waist and lifted her until they were eye to eye. He didn't say a word but captured her mouth with his. The kiss they shared wasn't chaste, but full of passion from a man that loved his woman. After what seemed liked hours, but was only a few minutes, Titus lowered Tosha to the ground.

"I better let you go so that I can get back into Pastor mode." Tosha stepped back and smirked.

"What mode are you in now, Pastor?" She asked flirtatiously?

"Girl, in the mode of a man in love and in need of his woman. So, I urge you to go while you can, and I remain a true man of the cloth. Can you please send Deacon Dewayne back in?"

"I will after I reapply my lipstick." Tosha grabbed her purse and went into his powder room to touch up her make-up. When she came out, her man in love was back to his pastoral persona and in his robe for service.

"Okay, I'm leaving. May the Lord bless the word you are about to give to his people." She said as she exited the room.

"Deacon Dewayne, you're needed," Tosha said as she approached Tina. Deacon Dewayne rushed in, no doubt trying to keep the timing of the service. She and Tina locked eyes and smiled like school girls as they headed to the sanctuary.

Titus was adjusting his robe and made his way to exit, but before Deacon Dewayne opened the door, there was a question he had to ask.

"Pastor, can I ask you something?"

"Sure."

"Why did you propose to your lady at church? Why not someplace more romantic?" Titus gave a sly smile and patted Deacon Dewayne on the shoulder.

"My friend, that woman makes me feels things I never felt before. This is Holy Ground, and I needed to remain holy. After we are married, don't you worry, we will not lack in romance." Deacon Dewayne smiled at his Pastor and opened the door. He escorted the Shepherd of Kingdom Building Ministries into the morning worship service.

Act·Four

Episode Seventeen

There was an anointing in the atmosphere as the choir went forth in songs of praise. They sang "Giants Do Fall" by Donald Lawrence while the liturgical ministry led the congregation in praise in the form of dance. The sermonic solo was led with such passion as Sister Trina sang Yolanda Adams' version of "The Battle is Not Yours but the Lord's." There was a spirit of praise and worship in the Kingdom Building Ministries' Sanctuary, and it was all in reverence to The Almighty.

On stage, Pastor Titus was kneeling in total submission to The God of All. Tosha had all but forgotten about the diamond ring she now wore and was filled with the Holy Spirit; her hands lifted in praise. There was a sweet spirit in the air, and it lasted throughout the worship hour.

Pastor Titus' message was confirmation to all that their battle was indeed the Lord's to fight as he taught from 1 Samuel 17:47. His subject was, when you turn your worry into worship, God will turn your battles into blessings. For the first time since the passing of Pearl, Titus gave the testimony of their love, trials, and the battle with breast cancer they ultimately lost. He told the congregation how he had worried that he might not be able to fulfill his calling or to have the natural blessings he desired in life, like a life partner and children. But God touched him and gave him the vision to honor Pearl's ministry with not just a Health Ministry, as they had before, but with a health clinic. He conveyed to them how that vision had led Dr. Tosha Dunson Hightower to enter his life. Pastor Titus asked for Dr. Hightower to come to the stage. Sister Tina escorted her up the stairs, and Pastor Titus took her hand and turned to the congregation.

"I know that most of you are aware that Dr. Hightower is the Director of our Pearl Health Ministry and Facility. However, this morning, on this Member's Appreciation Day, I want to introduce you to my bride-to-be, Sister Tosha Hightower."

There were gasps, stunned faces, but mostly applause and standing ovations. Tosha stood squeezing Titus' hand so tightly that her fingers were turning purple. She was not sure what to make of his announcement or the congregation's response, so she just smiled and waved with her free hand as her fiancée continued to speak.

"I know you all will treat the future Mrs. Smith with the utmost respect and will want to greet her today. We will be at the membership dinner after service for you to make her acquaintance. Now, there's a thousand of you out there. I don't want to run her off, so let's keep it brief." Titus turned to his love and kissed her on the cheek, then spoke. "Honey, it's okay for you to take your seat again now. I just wanted God's people to see that I am a living testimony that He won't leave you nor forsake you and that He. Is. A. God. Of. A. Second. Chance."

Episode Eighteen

Tosha had never hugged and spoken to so many people in her life. Everyone was trying to tell her how they grew up with Pastor and knew this and that about him and his family. It was quite overwhelming, but she remained gracious. At least, she hoped she did. Finally, it was time to be seated and for dinner to be served. Before going to the ladies' room, Tosha looked around for Tina to tell her, but she was speaking to someone else. Tosha recalled Titus informing her to allow Sister Tina to escort her where she needed to go. *That's silly.* She could go to the restroom and freshen up alone. She was a grown woman after all.

Tosha was washing her hands when she caught a glimpse of the last woman she wanted to see coming into the room striding toward her, followed by two ladies that had looks that could kill on their faces. Suddenly, she was regretting being alone but decided to be nice.

"Good Afternoon, Sister Barbara, and ladies. I don't think I have formally met you." Tosha smiled as she dried her hands and extended it to the ladies she had not met before. Her hand was left hanging as all three-woman, hands on their hips and lips poked out, stared at her with scowls on their faces.

In the calmest tone she could manage, Tosha asked, "Is there a problem, ladies?"

"Yes, the problem is you didn't take me seriously when I said you weren't getting him," Barbara answered.

The sister wearing a gaudy orange polka-dot dress and matching hat decided to give her two-cents. "We don't know what's wrong with Pastor bringing your uppity medical professionals up in here thinking y'all can be our first lady. He ought to see it ain't the Lord's will when Pearl died." Before Tosha could process Sister Polka Dots words, the third sister in a brown wool suit, too hot for the eighty-degree weather, added the icing on the get-Tosha-straight cake.

"Now, Barbara done spent the last year, cooking, cleaning, working for him, and being everything, and I mean, *everything* he needed in a woman."

"Wait a minute, Helen." Barbara stopped Sister Wool Suit from speaking and moved directly into Tosha's space. Barbara was at least a foot taller than Tosha. She peered down at her as she spoke.

"I have been giving Titus what he needed before Pearl, during Pearl, and after Pearl. I will expose it all before I step to the side and let you have him." With every ounce of strength Tosha had, she forced herself not to react. She moved out of Barbara's space and placed her paper towel in the garbage, grabbed her purse off the counter, and exited the restroom without saying a word.

In the hall, she saw a flabbergasted Tina. "Where have you been? I've been looking all over for you. Pastor Titus won't allow dinner to be served until you are seated."

"I had to use the restroom." Tina's attention went to the ladies' room doors as it opened and saw Barbara and her crew exiting. She frowned at them and looked to Tosha with concern.

"Did something happen in there with them?" Tosha gave a smile that didn't reach her eyes.

"Let's just say we had a meeting in the ladies' room." She took Tina by the hand. "Nothing to worry about. Let's go in and eat dinner."

Tina hesitantly went along, knowing that Pastor Titus was concerned about Tosha being alone. She could only pray Barbara and those messy friends of hers had not started anything foolish.

Episode Nineteen

Tosha was able to push Barbara's threats to the back of her mind. It was easy when she entered the fellowship hall that looked more like an elaborate ballroom with its red, white, and black color scheme. She took in the splendor of it all and felt a shiver go up her spine when she saw Titus's demeanor go from serious pastor to giddy fiancée when he looked her way. He ended the conversation he was having with a couple and walked toward her. Upon reaching her, he took her by the hands and gave her a friendly hug. He whispered, "I thought you had changed your mind."

Tosha looked up into his brown eyes and winked stating, "Never, you not going to be able to get rid of me." Titus smiled and escorted her and Tina to their table.

Tosha loved how their table was decorated just like all the others. There was no table set aside for those with titles. They all sat and ate among each other as the catering staff served the hundreds of diners. Everything was going well until Sister Barbara Stoneheart made her way to their table.

Tosha picked up her glass of sweet tea as Barbara made her way around their table greeting each person. She was a totally different person than the villain in the restroom. She hugged and cheek-kissed every man and woman at the table, except her. Tosha looked to Titus, as Barbara gave him a hug and then took the only vacant seat on the other side of him. *Did he not notice that Barbara hadn't spoken to her?* She locked eyes with Tina, and they both gave each other a this-female-is-crazy look, but Tosha continued to eat until Titus spoke up.

"Sister Barbara, did you congratulate my fiancée today?" Tosha was relieved. She didn't believe a word Barbara had said earlier, but she still had her eyes and ears open.

"Oh, Dr. Hightower and I spoke in the lady's room, Pastor Titus. Didn't we, sweetie?" Barbara looked around Titus to make eye contact with Tosha, who didn't return the gaze or answer the question. Barbara went on talking anyway.

"I was telling her that she could expect the same support from me as my dearly departed friend, Pearl, received. I let her know how I have always served you and that nothing will change between us going forward. You know me. I'm all about supporting and serving at Kingdom Building Ministries."

Titus got an uneasy feeling from Barbara's comments and could feel Tosha stiffen beside him. It wasn't lost on him that the other members at the tables had looks of disbelief on their faces. Barbara's tone was unnerving, but he thought she meant no harm.

"Sister Barbara, we have both been around this church since we were tots. I expect no less from you. We are here to serve the Lord until he calls us home. Since you are on the administrative team, I will go ahead and tell you that Sis. Tina will take the role of the Lady Elect Assistant."

Barbara's smile faded, and she gave a piercing look that she covered quickly with a faux smile. Titus didn't know what to make of it. He was relieved that Barbara stood to leave.

"Well, I guess congratulations are in order, Sister Douglas. I know you and Dr. Hightower were already friends. Pastor, I will see you in the morning when I report for my duties with you." With that, Barbara sashayed away feeling confident that she had planted a big seed of discord and doubt.

***

On the drive home, Titus had one hand on the steering wheel as he held Tosha's with the other. Her mood was not what he expected for a newly engaged woman that screamed yes earlier in his office. Maybe the day had been too much for her. He had to know.

"Sweetheart, is everything okay? You seem a little distant." He glanced at her briefly before focusing back on the road. Tosha sighed and turned her body to face his.

"Titus, we need to talk about Barbara Stoneheart." Titus glanced her way with a look of bewilderment.

"We need to talk about Barbara? Why?"

"Because, when I was in the restroom earlier today, she and two of her friends cornered me and read me my rights. They said I would not be their first lady and that Barbara would continue to meet all your needs. Then Barbara informed me that she had been meeting your *needs* in every way before Pearl, during Pearl, and after Pearl. She threatened to expose it all if we married."

Titus turned the car so sharply into the parking lot of a Kohl's that the tires screeched, and Tosha's seatbelt tightened to the point it was squeezing her. Titus put the car in park then turned off the ignition and looked at his future wife.

"Tosha, I don't know what sick game Barbara is playing but hear me well. I have *never* had sex with her or anyone except Pearl in the last fifteen years. Was I a virgin when I married Pearl? No, but I was saved and celibate for three years before I married her. I have never slept with Barbara. I have mistaken her as a friend, but that will be rectified." Titus pulled out his cell phone and placed a call.

"Hey, Deacon Dewayne, sorry, I'm going to have to disturb your evening after a long day. Please get Sister Yvette in human resources to meet us back at my office, and then have Sister Barbara Stoneheart and your wife attend. Barbara will be terminated effective immediately. Thanks, see you shortly."

Tosha was amazed. She knew Titus was alpha, but this put a capital *A* in Alpha. She leaned over and gave him a sweet kiss on the lips and said, "Thank you."

Titus held her chin in his hand and stated, "No one will hurt you or lie on me and remain in our lives. We are about to build something, and it must be on a firm foundation. Let's go take care of this, so I can take you back home to rest for your week."

Episode Twenty

The conference room off Pastor Titus's office was occupied by the pastor, Tosha, Barbara Stoneheart, Sister Yvette, the human resource coordinator, Deacon Dewayne, Sister Tina, and, to Tosha's surprise, Sister Polka Dot Dress, who was introduced as Liz Jefferson, and Sister Wool Suit, Helen Williams. The two additional ladies were called by Deacon Dewayne after Tina informed him she saw them coming out of the ladies' room with Barbara. Sister Yvette and Titus approved of them being in attendance as hostile witnesses Tosha assumed.

Pastor Titus began the meeting in prayer. After saying amen, he went into the purpose of the meeting. All in attendance had straight backs and eyes focused on the pastor as he spoke.

"I have called this meeting to address false statements that were made to my fiancée, Dr. Hightower, in the ladies' room. I approved Deacon Dewayne for all those in that discussion to be present. Sister Yvette is present because she represents the Human Resources Department for Kingdom Building Ministries. Deacon Dewayne and Sister Douglas are here because they are the Pastor's and Lady Elect's Executive Assistants. Are there any questions before we go further?"

Titus scanned the room. Some said, "No, Pastor," while others shook their heads no.

"Excellent. If time permitted, I would go into the book of Proverbs and point out all the reasons why it is to one's detriment to behave like a fool or keep company and take counsel from the foolish. However, the day has been blessed, but the hour is late. I implore you all to study the book of Proverbs and Matthew chapter four." Titus stroked his beard and took a drink out of his bottle of water.

"Sister Barbara, it has come to my attention that you, Sister Liz, and Sister Helen made accusations to my fiancée about the role you have played in my personal and romantic life. What I've heard are lies that I need to be cleared up immediately. I will not have anyone intimidating my lady, nor slandering my reputation just to cause strife for entertainment purposes." Titus looked at the three ladies, and they each felt like he could see through them to their souls. Sister Helen and Sister Liz were immediately convicted and spoke in unison.

"I'm sorry, Pastor." Both their voices were trembling and their eyes filled with tears. Titus nodded his head in satisfaction. "I accept your apology, but I'm not the only person you offended."

"I'm sorry for the things I said, Sister—um Dr. Hightower." Sis Liz said humbly.

"I am as well; I truly am sorry for the disrespect and for saying things I didn't know were true or not." Sis Helen said.

Tosha felt as though they were genuine, but then again, she couldn't be sure. They had apologized, so it was her duty to forgive them. She suspected they were just following Barbara's lead anyway. She smiled at them both and said, "I accept your apologies and hope you give me the opportunity to get to know you better, and you, me."

"Yes, ma'am, we would like that very much." They both practically sang in unison.

All eyes turned to Barbara, but if anyone in that conference room thought Barbara Stoneheart would follow this peaceful path, they were mistaken.

"Titus, what exactly did I lie about?" Barbara snapped her neck to look his way after seeing her so-called friends turn on her in a flash. She pointed at her chest while speaking.

"Have I not been your friend since we were kids? Did I not help Pearl get acclimated in the ministry? Did I not help her plan a wedding that should've been mine? When Pearl was diagnosed, I was by both your sides day and night, and never neglected my duties here at the church. Did I not allow you to cry on my shoulders at night for weeks until you went to sleep? Yes, I did that and more for you, and this is how you treat me? Bringing me in front of a committee like we are not practically family? If I offended Tosha because she misunderstood something I said, it was worth no more than a phone call, not all this mess." Barbara flung her arms around the table insulted that she had been called out in front of so many people. She folded her arms across her chest and gave her customary roll of the neck and eyes.

Titus hated dramatics and did not acknowledge tantrums. He was also stunned to hear how long Barbara had harbored feelings for him. *Had he been so blind all these years*? If he had known, Titus would have never introduced her to Pearl. But that was neither here nor there now. Barbara was out of line, and it was time to bring this confusion of hers to an end.

"Sister Stoneheart, I thought those deeds were done in the name of friendship, and you and I were never alone in my home. I have never given you any reason to believe you were the lady in my life. You may like to put this innocent spin on your malicious intent, but the Devil is a liar. Effective immediately, you are terminated from the

Pastoral Administration Staff based on insubordination and causing strife among the members of Kingdom Building Ministries. Sister Yvette will stay and complete your exit papers with you. Deacon Dewayne will escort you to your office for you to clear it out. You are to give him all your security passes to the administration facilities of this property. It is at your discretion if you would like to continue your membership here." Titus stood, prompting Tosha and Tina to stand as well.

"This meeting is adjourned." Titus took Tosha by the hand and exited the room. Sister Tina, Liz, and Helen followed, leaving Barbara Stoneheart to her doom.

Episode Twenty-One

Once again, Titus was en route to take Tosha home. They rode in silence, both in their own thoughts.

Titus hated that his proposal day had taken such an ugly turn, but he was not a man to let discord linger and have time to grow. He was deeply wounded that his childhood friend had created an illusion of them having a future and seething about the lies she told his lady that could have ended their relationship. However, this was not uncommon. He had counseled countless women who created a life in their mind and tried to will it into existence. He had one sister tell him she was calling things into existence that were not manifested yet. Too often, misinterpretation of Romans 4:17 led men and woman into delusional obsession. One cannot speak into existence another person to love them. In that sister's case, she was waiting on her husband who had put a restraining order on her for stalking. He shook his head at the thought of how that sister spiraled out of control and ended up doing time in jail for assaulting the object of her affection's fiancée. Her defense was that she was trying to move the mountain that was in her way. These cases were what caused him grief and agony being a leader in ministry. Souls that were lost could be prayed for, but the loss of a sound mind was the kind that needed prayer and fasting for any hope of deliverance. He could not let any such behavior go unaddressed in his congregation. Especially, against his love.

His love was watching his demeanor and could see he was troubled. Tosha touched his hand to bring him out of his reverie.

"Titus, are you okay?" He blinked out of his thoughts and took her hand and kissed the back of it.

"Yes, I'm fine. I was just thinking about the mind and how fragile it is." Then he glanced her way, and she could see the love and concern in his eyes.

"Tosha, I'm sorry our engagement day has such an ugly stain on it. Maybe I should have waited to address the issue tomorrow, but that is not the type of leader I am, or man. I confront things head on. I hope today hasn't made you think twice about marrying me." It was Tosha's turn to give him a look of love.

"Titus, I'm a surgical oncologist. I am trained to encourage patients to fight cancer cells immediately. If they don't, the cells spread to other organs in the body and then the battle becomes that much harder to win. I know you understand this from experience, but from a doctor viewing the onset of cancer, it going untreated because the patient and their family are in shock or denial is alarming. Because I know the patient is allowing the cancer cells time to take root in their body and giving the disease the opportunity to spread throughout." Tosha took a deep breath as she thought about a special patient, Olivia Harvey. She was a perfect example.

"Take for instance a patient I'm seeing tomorrow. She is a young single mother who started with a small bone tumor. She didn't want to do chemotherapy because of the side effects and there being no one to care for her daughter. It's now a year later. In addition to bone cancer, there is a possibility she will soon be in hospice, dying of lung cancer. Because of her delay to undergo treatment, the cancer cells spread to her lungs and the treatments were too late to give her a chance of remission."

Tosha could normally hold her emotions together, but the outcome of this case could have been different if Olivia had agreed to treatment in the early stages. Titus gave her hand a gentle squeeze, and she continued, "Her daughter is in foster care. Sister Survivors helped her get placed in a loving home, and the foundation sends the foster family a donation for her daughter's needs monthly. The little girl is so beautiful and smart. I wish I could adopt her."

Tosha stopped speaking because that patient and her daughter meant the world to her. She was fighting back the tears but wanted to get her point across and not get sidetracked by her own desires.

They had made it to her home and were now parked in her driveway. Titus was now able to give her his undivided attention. Tosha stroked the side of his face with her hand. He melted at her touch, and she spoke words of comfort and encouragement to him. "Titus, I have a new respect and deeper love for you because of your reaction when I told you what Barbara said. You saw it as the cancer cell it was. You treated it right away so that it would not have a chance to set-up division in our relationship or the ministry. You have more than proved to me that I'm making the right decision in agreeing to be your wife." Tosha leaned in and gave him a sweet kiss on the lips. Titus took her into his arms as best he could with the divider between them and hugged her, kissing her on the forehead. Without anything further being said, he got out of the car, walked around to the passenger side, and opened the door for his lady. He helped her out, escorted her to her front door, gave her a final hug then stood at the door until he heard the lock turn ensuring her safety.

He got back in his car and lifted his eyes unto heaven and said, "Thank you, Lord, for sending me love again."

Episode Twenty-Two

"I know, Mom, it's not that. The time was right, and I went for happiness." Titus listened attentively as his mother voiced her displeasure about him becoming engaged to a woman she hadn't met in person. He nodded his head as if she could see him. He respected his mother and didn't like upsetting her.

"Mother, I understand, listen to me. You have been in Haiti for ten months. Life can be conceived and birthed in that time frame, and I have found love again. You are going to love Tosha. She is a wonderful woman." Titus rubbed his hand through his curly hair. He went from bald to a head full of curly locks depending on his mood. After Pearl had died, he shaved his black locks of curls off in lament. Since meeting and dating Tosha, he had let it grow out into a low, curly afro. Tosha said she loved it, and he would be keeping it this way until they married. However, his mother, Eunice, was about to make him pull some of it out. She wasn't getting that he could not stop his life because she was on a mission trip. Eunice had planned the year long trip three years ago before Pearl was diagnosed with Breast Cancer. She tried to back out of it after Pearl passed, but Titus wouldn't allow it. Now, Eunice was sure she should have stayed because her son was rebounding and about to marry a stranger. She was letting him know she wasn't having it.

"Mother, it's done—I'm sure this is right. I love her in a way that is new to me. I'm not rebounding. I was a faithful husband to Pearl unto death, but I'm alive, and

Tosha is heaven sent. Now someone is knocking at my door. I promise we will Skype soon and you can meet her that way. I love you and goodbye." Titus ended the call. Maybe he should have told his mother about Tosha after date one, but what was done was done. She would love Tosha; he just knew it. Titus heard another knock on his door and said, "Come in."

Deacon Dewayne and Sister Yvette walked in with distressed looks. Titus raised an eyebrow at their pensive faces. Both sat down in the matching chairs flanking his massive desk.

"You two look like you lost your best friends. What's troubling my best employees?" Titus stroked his chin as he waited for one of them to respond. Deacon Dewayne went first.

"Well, Pastor, it seems that Sister Barbara is not going to depart the church as a member."

Titus shrugged. He had left that entirely up to Barbara. He still cared about her soul though she was no longer an employee, that was that.

"That has you both in this state? Sis Barbara continuing her membership?" Titus looked between his two closest administrators, hoping there was more. Sister Yvette spoke up.

"Sir, it's not just her remaining a member. She has contacted some of the trustees saying she had been wrongfully terminated. Deacon Dewayne and I are receiving phone calls from the board inquiring about her being fired." Titus didn't respond he just moved in closer to his desk, placing his elbows on top and lacing his fingers under his chin, urging Yvette to continue with a head nod. Yvette switched positions in her seat. Her mouth had become dry. She could see the Pastor didn't understand the urgency of the matter. She cleared her throat to continue, while Deacon Dewayne all but pleaded with his eyes to make the Pastor comprehend what was going on.

"Of course, we are within the church bylaws and the state of Tennessee's At Will employment law to terminate her as an employee. But, it's not just the board. Sister Barbara is on several auxiliaries here, and she has contacted hundreds of members saying she was fired because Sister Tosha didn't like her and the relationship she had with you." Titus frowned as wrinkles formed across his forehead.

"You have got to be kidding me. I couldn't care less what lies she is spreading to busy bodies. This is nothing but nonsense." Yvette closed her eyes. Pastor Titus was a no-nonsense man. She feared he wouldn't see how busybodies could destroy what he was building at KBM. Deacon Dewayne knew it too.

"Pastor, we agree they are busybodies, but an empty wagon makes the most noise. There has been plenty of talk about how we are hiring outside the fold in the health facility. We don't want Sister Barbara's lies to add more fuel to the fire."

Titus did not understand their concerns. In a church KBM's size, he had accepted he would not be able to make everyone happy. He made sure they followed the church bylaws, state laws, and the word of God in all his church administration. He would not be detoured or stop to address utter foolishness.

"Sister Yvette, we posted the available jobs in the church directory, correct?"

"Yes, sir."

"We terminated Sister Barbara within the law of the church and state. You just confirmed that, right?"

"Yes, sir."

"So, there is nothing the board can say we did wrong, is that correct?" He looked at both Yvette and Dewayne. The both nodded their heads in the affirmative. Titus leaned back in his chair appearing to be in a more relaxed state. Although he felt a headache coming on, he didn't let on to his employees.

"So, what is it that you two feel I should be concerned about, and what do you want me to do about it?"

Yvette gave Dewayne a look that said she had nothing. Pastor Titus made her feel as if she came in screaming the sky was falling when there wasn't any movement on Earth.

"Pastor, I think you should call a meeting with the congregation or at least the committees that Sister Barbara is on to nip this in the bud." Titus gave him an incredulous look.

"You want me to call a meeting to address a former employee's lies? Not a chance. I am not about to waste the good people of KBM's time on nonsense. I have served with an open heart. The members who love the Lord and are committed know my heart. I am not concerned about those who are only following for entertainment and for the fish and loaves we give out." Titus waved the notion off with his hand. "Is there anything else we need to discuss?"

In defeat, Yvette and Dewayne answered in unison. "No, Pastor." They both stood and exited the office.

Titus opened his desk drawer and pulled out a bottle of aspirin and sighed.

"Lord, will you help me?"

Episode Twenty-Three

It was a Monday full of the blues. Tosha woke up with cramps from her cycle that made her want to crawl underneath the bed and hide from the rain that was falling outside. But she woman upped and pushed forward with what was on her agenda for the day. She did her morning routine slowly, but she got it all in, prayer time, bicycling that helped her symptoms, and dressing for work. When she put on her new engagement ring, she couldn't help but smile at the thought of a future with Titus.

She was mesmerized by the alpha male who had captured her heart, intrigued by his aptitude in all things of culture, and inspired by his spiritual strength and the reverence he had for the Lord. Titus was everything she wanted and already provided things she didn't know she needed. Yesterday, he proved to her that she could trust him with her heart, and reputation. And the very thought of giving him her body made her blush, standing in her bathroom alone. Before she could even start planning her wedding or see the man that had captured her heart, she had to make it through the day.

Today, she was to consult with Olivia Harvey's medical team. Olivia had entered the last stage of cancer, and Tosha feared that the results of all the scans would lead to Olivia being placed in hospice. This hurt Tosha deeply. She had developed a bond with Olivia and wanted her to beat the cancer and raise her little girl Summer, but that would only be possible if a miracle happened. Tosha believed in miracles, but the realities of biology and science kept her grounded in facts. Olivia would not likely see the end of the year alive, and Summer would be in permanent foster care. With those dreary thoughts hanging low like the clouds she drove through to reach the hospital, Tosha's blues kicked in full force causing her spirits to become low.

A few hours later, what the meteorologist had predicted to just be light rain throughout the day had progressed into a severe thunderstorm. The skyline was dark as night in the early afternoon. There were multiple wrecks on Interstate Two-Forty that caused Tosha to be stuck in stand-still traffic with Olivia Harvey. They had received the results of her latest scans, and Tosha's fears were confirmed; Olivia was being placed in hospice. There was nothing else medically to be done. The cancer had won. Tosha was taking Olivia to The Hospice House, but before going there, they were going to see Summer. They sat in silence as the lighting flashed and the thunder roared. Tosha and Olivia looked on as the Tennessee Department of Transportation workers assisted motorist involved in another wreck. The windshield wipers were on high and the sound of them screeching against the windshield, barely allowing Tosha any visibility, was annoying and grated on Tosha's patience. The pain in her abdomen was real, but she could not let cramps break her down into a crying mess like she wanted to do. This day utterly sucked. She was no weakling, and she would not let period cramps break her when she was in the presence of Olivia, who was literally on her death bed and had never uttered one complaint. When she did speak, Olivia startled Tosha who was lost in her own discomfort.

"Did you hear me, Dr. Hightower?" Olivia said with the weakest voice Tosha had ever heard. Tosha leaned to the side to hear her while keeping her eyes on the road. Traffic had started to move as soon as Olivia spoke.

"I'm sorry, what did you say?"

"I said, do you think your new fiancée will let you raise Summer?" Tosha looked over to Olivia, taking her eyes off the road.

BAM! It was that quick. Tosha hit the vehicle in front of her. Both airbags inflated as glass shattered from the impact of the crash. It was a Monday full of the blues, Tosha thought as the pressure in her temple caused her to lose consciousness slowly.

Episode Twenty-Four

Titus was sitting in a community meeting for Pastors discussing an upcoming joint revival. The plans were being headed by Pastor Andre Jefferson of Holy Tabernacle. Titus had already agreed to speak one night, and KBM would donate the refreshments for two of the five-night revival. He began filtering through his emails and grimaced when he saw the Senior Trustee had called an emergency meeting. He did not want to have to address Barbara Stoneheart's termination again, but it looked like he wouldn't be able to avoid it. Accepting the meeting that Dewayne had sent him to add to his schedule, he was lost in thought and did not notice that Dewayne had entered the meeting and was asking for him. Hearing his name called out, with what seemed to be panic in Dewayne's voice, he apologized for the disruption and made a quick exodus out of the conference room behind the deacon. When they were in the hallway, Dewayne filled him in.

"Pastor, Sis Annabelle called and said she received a call from Janine Owens, who introduced herself as

Tosha's first cousin. She said this Janine person said Tosha had been in a car wreck and is in the emergency room at the Regional One." Titus stood there stunned at first trying to process what Dewayne had said. His heart and mind were not wired to accept such news the day after his engagement became official. He was in a trance until Dewayne touched him on the shoulder.

"Pastor, we need to get to the hospital."

***

Tosha was getting dressed. The nurse had given Tosha her discharge papers. She had fainted in the car for some unknown reason that an MRI could not determine. She only had small scratches on her face from shattered glass and a bruise from the airbag. The silver lining on this Monday of blues was the Demerol that was administered to her. That great invention made her menstrual cloud of blues all roll away. Her cousin Janine was listed in her phone as ICE, in case of emergency. Janine came as soon as she could with her twin daughters, Hope and Charity. Tosha had Janine call Titus who was now storming into her room.

He burst in the room panting as if he had run the entire way to her bedside. Titus took Tosha by both hands and stared at her from head to toe. Tosha couldn't be certain, but she thought he counted her fingers to make sure all ten were there. When he was happy with his examination results, Titus pulled her into a tight embrace and kissed her on the forehead. Then, and only then, was he able to exhale.

"I don't know what I would've done if you were hurt," he whispered in her ear as he applied kisses to each scratch and bruise on her beautiful face. Tosha pulled away as she could see her cousin turning beet red.

"Titus, honey, I'm okay. I may experience some soreness, but right now, I am fine." She motioned toward Janine who sat in the only chair in the room.

"Please, meet my first cousin Janine Owens. I've told you about her and the girls, Hope and Charity." Titus couldn't believe he had not noticed them in the room. His sole focus was on his lady. He went over and shook Janine's hand in a friendly shake.

"Thank you so much for being there for Tosha, Janine. It's a pleasure to meet you and these two beautiful angels. Tosha has told me quite a bit about you and your husband, Seth. Hopefully, we can get together soon."

"It's a pleasure to meet you in person, Pastor Smith. I have followed your ministry for years now and couldn't be happier that you are with Tosha." Janine looked at her cousin and was truly happy for her.

"Tosha, since Pastor Titus—"

Titus interrupted, "No, you are family. Call me Titus."

Janine smiled. "Very well, since you are here, *Titus*, I'm going to take these two little girls home to put them down for their nap."

"No, mommy, we not sleepy." Charity, the outspoken twin, protested. Titus and Tosha laughed. Janine shook her head in exasperation and bent down eye-level to her daughter. "Yes, Charity, we are going home, and you will take a nap, understand?" Charity understood but didn't like it. She nodded her *yes* in agreement. She did not want a time-out, or worse, a spanking. Janine hugged Tosha and Titus one last time, followed by hugs from the twins, and left Tosha in the capable of hands of her man.

Titus turned around to access Tosha again. He was so grateful she was not injured. He wasn't sure if he could have survived it. "I'm so happy you are okay. Let's get you home so you can take a nice long bath and relax."

"That sounds wonderful, but we have to check on Olivia first." Bewildered, Titus looked down at her.

"I thought you consulted with her team today?"

"I did, and we were en route to allow her to see her daughter, Summer, and then take her to hospice." Titus' heart went out to Tosha. He knew how hard that was for her. He could see it in her chocolate irises. He pulled her into another hug.

"Oh, sweetheart, I'm sorry. I didn't know she was with you. Of course, we will check on her." He reached for her hand and started to walk out of the room. Titus looked behind him because he felt Tosha pulling back. He turned to observe her.

"What is it? Do you need something else from the nurse? I can push you in the wheelchair. It's right outside the room."

"No, it's not that. Olivia asked me a question that startled me, and I looked away from the road." Titus looked concerned as Tosha's gaze fell to the floor. He lifted her chin up with his index finger.

"What did she ask you?"

"If my new fiancée will allow me to raise her daughter, Summer?" Tosha was shocked that Titus didn't seem to react to the question, not even a blink.

"Is that something you want?"

Tosha fidgeted which was so unlike her. This was the first request she was making of her fiancée, and it was a life-changer.

"Yes, it is, but I understand if it's too much to ask."

"There is nothing you can't ask of me. Let's go see Olivia, and we will discuss our options." Tosha reached up and gave Titus a warm kiss on the lips. This man was sent from God, and, just like that, a Monday full of rain and blues was turned into a day of sunshine.

Episode Twenty-Five

It was five o'clock on Tuesday morning, Titus was in his home gym in the basement. Most homes in his area did not have a basement, but it was a must for him. When he and the architect designed his home, which was in Southeast Shelby County in an exclusive gated community, he made sure the underground room was on the blueprint.

Titus had petitioned the Father for direction for him and Tosha concerning Summer. Meeting Olivia the day before had touched him deeply and reopened some of the wounds he would forever have after losing Pearl. Olivia had given them a copy of her living will, which indeed listed Tosha as the child's desired caregiver. He appreciated Tosha telling Olivia that they would pray and let her know soon.

Titus was now doing his circuit workout, which started with him bench pressing one hundred and eighty-five pounds until he felt the burn. Today, it would take longer because his mind continually drifted back to the evening before, when he met Summer, who was a beautiful and well-mannered little girl.

Titus, watching Summer embrace her mother with tears streaming down her face, telling Olivia that the Angels were going to watch over her all night, melted his heart like butter over fire. The young girl was smart and loving, and she was happy to see Tosha. His lady could not hold back the tears as she talked with Summer and watched the mother and daughter spend what could very well be their last time together. He wanted nothing more but to take Summer away from the foster home that night to live with him or Tosha until they were married. However, he knew he must acknowledge the Lord and allow His will to be done.

As he moved to the squat section and began another rigorous regime, he prayed out loud. "Lord, lead us in the way you would have us to go. We don't want to be moved by emotions but by your spirit. You know the battle

Summer will face. Please direct us if we are the parents that can help her grow into the young lady you would have her to be. In Jesus name, amen."

Now, doing pull ups, he grunted with each lift, as he subjected his body to a grueling workout. He often worked out, putting his flesh to the test, when he sought the Lord for guidance. To Titus, it was like killing his flesh so his spirit could be stronger and more receptive to the voice of the Lord. Titus never mentioned this to anyone. It was his own personal prayer closet. He ended his workout with twenty minutes of high-speed jump roping. A peace settled into him about moving forward with marriage and the adoption of Summer. When he was in the shower, he thanked the Lord for always being there and asked him to be there for Tosha and Summer as Olivia made her transition to be with Him.

***

The passage of a few hours found Titus sitting at the desk in his office at KBM. He picked up his landline and called Tosha.

"Hello."

"Hi, sweetheart, how are you?"

"I'm well, just another busy day. How is your day going?"

"I've been in deep thought and prayer concerning our impending nuptials and family." Titus could hear Tosha holding her breath as she gasped on the other end of the phone. Her gasp let him know that adopting Summer was what she wanted.

"I agree that we should move forward in making our little girl, legally our daughter."

"Really!" Tosha yelled through the phone causing Titus to have to switch her to the speaker.

"Are you sure? I understand if—"

"Tosha, darling, I'm sure. We need to set our wedding date as soon as you are ready so we can start the process, and we need to do all that we can while Olivia is still with us." Tosha, smiling through her tears and nodding her head on the phone as though Titus could see her, was overwhelmed with emotions but gathered herself as best she could. She took a deep breath.

"I'll contact my family attorney immediately. Thank you, Titus, I love you."

Titus was stunned as he heard the dial tone, then he let out a heartfelt laugh. Tosha had hung up on him no doubt to start her calls. Titus pulled up his calendar on

Outlook and saw it was time for his meeting with the trustees. He was certain this meeting would have him feeling anything but great. He didn't mention it to Tosha because she had enough on her plate. He would deal with the Barbara Stoneheart drama on his own.

***

"Pastor, with all due respect, we understand Sister Barbara ruffled Dr. Hightower's feathers, but she is going to have to get used to it. That comes with being a pastor's wife. You can't expect her to get even half the respect Sister Pearl received. Especially when she just got here."

Brother John Edwards spoke with a definitive tone as some of the other board members nodded in agreement. Titus had listened to all their pitches on the restore-Barbara Stoneheart campaign, and it was time this meeting came to an end. He stood from his seat at the conference table, and all the men sat up and gave him the attention his six-foot-three frame commanded.

"Brethren, I agreed to this meeting out of respect for your positions as trustees. I value your dedication, input, and sacrifice to KBM. However, you must respect my decision when it comes to the employees of the business administration." Titus pressed his pointer finger on the table as he lowered his body to make eye contact with the men.

"No one will be paid to intimidate my lady. Although I understand that I can't make people like her, they will show her respect or deal with the consequences. Tosha is not here to fill Pearl's shoes. She wears her own. Our love is real, and she will not be tested by petty people. Barbara Stoneheart will not be reinstated on the staff, and that is final. I suggest you make the auxiliary leaders aware of my position regarding my fiancée or I will have new leaders and new board members. Good day, gentleman, meeting adjourned." Titus exited the office leaving all in attendance dumbfounded.

Episode Twenty-Six

The next couple weeks went by in a flash for Titus and Tosha. They were knee deep in paperwork trying to gain custody of Summer. It was all made possible by Olivia's will to live until her daughter was legally in Tosha's care. They had come to an agreement to allow Tosha to become the legal guardian, and after she became Dr. Smith, they would legally adopt Summer. To both their satisfaction, the church drama had faded away as quickly as it came.

Titus was prayerful that Barbara had accepted that there was no relationship between them other than that of Pastor and member, but deep in his gut, Titus felt she was still plotting. He kept her lifted in prayer, as did he pray for his mother who was soon to return. He had no idea how she would accept becoming a grandmother. However, he did not let any of these things stop his progression with Tosha and Summer. They spent time with Summer each night and allowed her to see Olivia every day. Everything was going smoothly, and they were all excited to see Olivia the night Summer legally became Tosha's. They just knew she would be elated that her final wish had been granted.

Titus, Tosha, and Summer walked hand in hand into The Hospice House to share the good news. Upon entering Olivia's room, Titus could sense the spirit of death. But he also saw a determined soul fighting death off to the bitter end. Olivia Harvey was a living miracle in the flesh, despite the fact that she was now mere bones, a skeleton of her previous self of just weeks ago. Per her nurse, most patients in her condition wouldn't have made it through the last forty-eight hours.

Once in Olivia's room, Summer broke free and ran to her mother's bedside.

"Momma, guess what? I can live with Ms. Tosha! She said it's of-fi—" Summer looked over her shoulder to get help with the word.

Tosha chimed in, "It's official, sweetheart."

She and Titus had both taken seats and watched Summer animatedly tell Olivia about the future she was going to have as a Smith. Olivia looked on with weary eyes and a faint smile. When Summer was finished, she climbed up into the bed and snuggled in the crux of her mother's arm. Olivia called out to Tosha and Titus.

"Can you two come closer?" she said in nothing more than a light whisper. They both hurried to her bedside, and she reached out both her hands. Titus took one hand and Tosha the other, while Summer lay on her mother's beating heart. With the little strength Olivia had, she squeezed both their hands saying, "Thank you . . . so . . . much. Now, I . . . can . . . rest . . . in . . . peace." She leaned back on the pillow and took in the couple and her daughter. She knew everything would be okay. While still holding the hands of her daughter's salvation and her little girl nestled on her one remaining breast, Olivia Harvey transitioned to glory.

Act·Five

Episode Twenty-Seven

It was the first Sunday of a new month and four weeks had passed since Olivia was laid to rest. Today was the debut of Summer Harvey to KBM. Titus and Tosha thought it best to allow Summer to adjust to her new life before adding the church layer on it. They had not kept Summer a secret, but there had been no formal announcement to the congregation. Titus would be doing that today at the end of service. He would also be sharing his wedding date, which would occur in six weeks. He and Tosha had prayed and fasted for seven days, and both agreed, it was time to become a family living under one roof. They had made other decisions that would require a great sacrifice from Tosha, according to Titus. She had decided to no longer do consults with oncology teams. She would focus on being a wife, mother, and director of The Pearl Health Ministry. Titus vowed to love her in such a mighty way, so she would never regret joining her life with his.

Tosha didn't see it so much as a sacrifice. After all, she now would have the best of all worlds. And it wasn't like she was going home to be barefoot and pregnant. Although, she was anxious to have her first biological child. The Lord, through Titus, was granting her heart's every desire. There was nothing she wanted more than the upcoming six weeks to pass by swiftly. So, on this Sunday morning, as she drove with Summer in the backseat of her Audi, she sang along with Yolanda Adams' "Victory." She couldn't be happier.

That happiness was attacked as soon as she stepped in the foyer of KBM. She was holding Summer's hand explaining to her that she would first go to Sunday School class, then she would get to see Daddy Titus. Summer started calling him Daddy Titus and her Momma Tosha out of the blue, and they were fine with it. Only, Summer did not like the order of events.

"Momma Tosha, I want to see Daddy Titus now. I want him to see me dressed up first. I don't want to wait," Summer whined. She was head over heels for her Daddy Titus, and Tosha couldn't blame her. But, their new little five-year-old daughter was going to have to obey.

Tosha opened her mouth to explain before she heard, "Well, Well. What do we have here?"

Tosha and Summer both looked around for the person who owned that wicked sounding voice. Tosha rolled her eyes when she saw Barbara Stoneheart and squeezed Summer's hand so tightly the child squealed.

"Momma Tosha, my hand hurts!" Tosha loosened her grip and pulled Summer into her waist.

"Good Morning, Sister Barbara," Tosha said trying to sound genuine only to receive a grimace from Barbara.

"Well, good morning to you too. I see you roped him in without revealing you were a ready-made family. How clever and common of you."

Tosha could not believe this woman's nerve. Didn't she get fired the last time she stepped to her incorrectly, and now this?

"Sis Barbara, this is my daughter, Summer. Please excuse us while I get her to Sunday School class. Enjoy the rest of your Sunday." Tosha turned to walk away not wanting to be in Barbara's presence any longer, but Summer had other ideas.

"No! No class first. I want to see Daddy—" Out of all the times, Summer chose this second to call Titus simply *Daddy*. Tosha watched Barbara's face turn two shades darker, and her eyes bulged out like Beetlejuice. Tosha had no choice but to change direction and head toward Titus's office.

"Okay, Okay. Settle down. We'll go see him." That satisfied Summer and the waterworks came to an end, but Tosha had a migraine coming on. She walked away, dragging Summer along and did not look back at Barbara. This was not how she wanted their daughter introduced. Tosha had no doubt Barbara would be starting the rumor mill about Summer without having one truthful fact.

***

Titus was reading over his notes for his sermon when he heard a knock on his office door. He wondered where Deacon Dewayne was for someone to have to knock.

"Come in." When he saw who was entering, his heart skipped a beat, and he jumped to his feet.

"Surprise! Are you happy to see me?"

"Of course, I'm happy to see my mother. Why did you end your trip early?" Titus grabbed his mother off her feet with a bear hug. He didn't realize how much he missed her until he laid eyes on her. She was thinner than before but still as beautiful as ever.

"My time was over there. I felt like I was needed here." Titus motioned for his mother to sit down on the couch, and he sat next to her.

"Mother, you are always needed here, but that was great work you were doing. Nevertheless, I am thrilled to have you home."

"I am thrilled to be home, and can't wait to hear my baby boy preach the word again." Titus blushed like a true momma's boy. A knock at the door was heard. "Excuse me, Mother, let me get the door. I have no clue were Deacon Dewayne is."

As Titus got up to walk toward the door, his mother murmured, "That's why I'm back. You need a better assistant. Where is my goddaughter, Barbara?"

Titus didn't answer his mother. Instead, he opened the door and had to take a step back to catch Summer as she jumped in his arms.

"Daddy Titus!"

"Hey, pumpkin. How are you?"

"I'm fine now that Momma Tosha let me see you."

"Well, I am better now that I see you both." Titus adjusted Summer in one arm as he pulled Tosha in for a kiss on the cheek with his other hand. "And how are you, beautiful?" Tosha sighed.

"Tired already." Titus gave her a questioning look, but his attention was drawn away when Eunice interrupted by walking over to them.

"Well, who and what do we have here?" Eunice looked at the trio with a scowl.

"Pardon my manners, Mother, but please, meet my beautiful fiancée, Dr. Tosha Hightower. This pumpkin is our daughter, Summer Harvey, soon to be Summer Smith."

Like the drama queen Eunice could be when the world was not tilting toward her axis, she passed out at their feet.

Episode Twenty-Eight

Titus could not believe his mother pulled her old antics of passing out. She did it for years with his father. He lowered Summer to her feet and helped his distraught mother up.

"Mom, please don't do this. Tosha and Summer are my world, my family." Eunice gave him a deer in the headlight stare and allowed him to walk her back to the couch. She was fanning herself as if she was experiencing a hot flash.

"Son, I don't mean to be rude, but this is a lot for a woman to take. I leave my son mourning his wife. I come back just months later, and he is getting remarried to a woman with a child. Titus, what will the members think? What does Barbara have to say about this?"

"Ooh, Momma Tosha, is Barbara that mean lady in the hall?" Summer asked. It appeared that Summer picked up the same vibes Tosha did from that woman. Tosha was in a state of shock. Summer had a discerning spirit and bluntness about her that had to be curbed. "Yes, sweetie, but it's not nice to call adults mean."

"So, Barbara's here," Eunice stated not caring that she had yet to acknowledge her future daughter-in-law and granddaughter.

"Yes, Mother. Barbara is here but only as a member."

"What do you mean only as a member? Did she quit because you took up with her?" Eunice pointed her finger toward Tosha like she was a piece of trash. Tosha had no clue how to respond. What she did know—she was done viewing this mess.

"Titus, I'm am going to take Summer home. You need to take care of this with your mother, and I suppose Barbara. We will see you later." Titus snapped his head toward Tosha.

"You will not be leaving, Tosha. Nothing has changed. Mother, you need to apologize to my fiancée and daughter at once." He gave his mother a stern look that meant he was not playing.

The only problem was—Eunice wasn't either.

"Who do you think you are talking to? I am your mother, and this is ridiculous. I left Barbara here to take care of you and finally, to get her chance at the spot she deserved. Now you done hooked up with a woman you think is some angel, but clearly is nothing but a loose woman with an illegitimate child."

That was it. Tosha had never jumped on anyone in her life, but before she knew it, she was flying across the room and slapped Eunice across the face. Titus grabbed her while Eunice fell backward on the couch, and Summer burst into tears. At that moment, Deacon Dewayne entered the room and saw the chaos. Titus turned to him barking orders.

"Dewayne, take my mother out." Dewayne rushed to do just that, not believing Pastor Titus was holding a still swinging Tosha by the waist. He could only assume the introductions did not go as planned.

Episode Twenty-Nine

"Tosha, calm down! What is wrong with you?" Titus' anger and frustration with the morning's events were at an all-time high. Tosha was pacing back and forth in front of him, ranting about what she was not going to stand for. Titus' interruption only made her angrier. She twirled around to face him.

"What's wrong with me?" Tosha pointed at her chest then at the office door. "Your mother, Barbara, who seemed to be the next runner up for the wife title, the rumors, the stares . . . That is what is wrong with me! Titus, I am a doctor. Do you know what it takes to come from the ghetto and become an oncologist? I have given my *life* to helping others and to be continually treated like trash is a bit much. But, I can take it because I know who I am. However, someone attacking Summer, that sweet innocent girl, is not something that I will tolerate." Tosha took a seat in one of the office chairs, buried her face in her hands, and wept. Titus' heart softened. He walked over to her and dropped to his knees in front of her, pulling her hands from her face and wiping her tears.

"Sweetheart, I understand that I have thrust you into a world that you are not used to. I appreciate you standing by and agreeing to become one with me. I love you and Summer with all my heart. There is no runner up for that love or to be my wife. But what can't happen again is you losing your cool and assaulting my mother or anyone else. That is beneath you and unacceptable. My mother was out of line, and I will deal with her. You just showed our daughter something I won't tolerate—violence will not happen in this relationship or from you."

"Titus, you should have let me leave. That is how I deal. I walk away when I feel angry, but you didn't let me. I know that is the wrong example, and if this has caused you to rethink being with me, I understand." Titus put his finger to Tosha's lips to silence her.

"Don't go there, Tosha. Nothing is changing between us because of this day. I will know to let you walk away to get in a calmer state, but there is no running home to hide. I was going to correct Mother, but you beat me to it. You must know that I wouldn't have let her insults stand. I love you, and Summer is my daughter. In hindsight, I should have announced the dynamics of our relationship to her sooner." Titus raised up and pulled Tosha up with him. "Sweetheart, I will make this right. Mother will apologize to you and Summer. We will get Summer from

Sister Tina and explain what happened today. Then we will go and worship the Lord, and I will speak to God's people and make the announcements as planned." He kissed her on the forehead and looked in her eyes searching for her reaction. "Is that okay with you?"

Tosha nodded yes while hugging him and sobbing into his chest. "I'm sorry, Titus. I will apologize. I wonder what Summer thinks of me. I'm going to be a terrible mother." The magnitude of her offense had registered with her, and she was ashamed. Titus could feel it as she trembled in his arms. He brushed her hair down and spoke to her lovingly.

"Sweetie, our little girl is a firecracker herself. She looked like she wanted you to hit Mother again. She knows you were defending her, and she now knows you have her back." Titus chuckled. "Now, please stop crying. Go to the restroom and freshen up. I'll be back in a few." Tosha nodded okay and retreated to his restroom. Titus left his office looking for his mother.

Episode Thirty

Titus had barely made it down the hall before he had to stop and greet members who were on their way to Sunday School class or to the meet and greet breakfast. He gave each member the time they needed to tell him who to pray for or to smile at the pictures on their phones of children and grandchildren. It was all part of the job. He truly cared for each member, but he had a family catastrophe to get under control.

His attention was taken away from Sister Washington who was showing him how proud she was of her grandson, Patrick, who was enrolled at Middle Tennessee State University and had made Dean's list his first semester. Titus knew the young man and was proud of him, and his accomplishments, but he had to excuse himself as Deacon Dewayne called for him. When he turned in that direction, he saw that the Deacon and Sister Tina were escorting Tosha's cousins Janine and Seth with their twin daughters his way. He felt relief and agony at once. Relief because Tosha had family support, but agony because they would know his mother was against the marriage. But no one could see the inner turmoil he was going through because Titus could smile through any trial.

"Good Morning, Brother and Sister Owens, I am so happy you agreed to join us today. Tosha will be happy you made it." Titus greeted Seth with a handshake and hugged Janine. He kissed Charity and Hope on their tiny little hands, and they giggled like he pulled a rabbit out of a hat.

"We're happy to share in this joyous occasion," Seth said.

"Where are Tosha and Summer?" Janine asked.

"She is in my study. Sister Tina and Deacon DeWayne will escort you all there. I have to see about another matter, and I will join you back there in a few minutes," Titus said with his charming smile, and then he went to his mother's office on the Foreign Missions' hall.

Entering his mother's office, Titus was not surprised to find her filling Barbara in on the morning's activities. The two were talking a mile a minute, and he had to clear his throat for his presence to be acknowledged. They looked his way and wore the same scowl on their faces.

"Sister Barbara, if you would excuse me. I would like to have a word with my mother."

"No, she will not be excused, Titus. You have some explaining to do. You have fired Barbara, a woman that has served you for years, over foolishness." Eunice was livid when Barbara told her all that had transpired in her absence.

"Now, son, I know grief can be hard to get through, and it's clear you are not over Pearl." Titus raised his hand to stop her talking.

"Mother, you stop right there. Don't bring Pearl into any conversation to excuse your behavior." Titus looked to Barbara again and stated firmer. "Sister Barbara, please excuse us." Barbara made a motion to stand up from her chair. She wasn't ready to tangle with Titus, but Eunice pulled her back down to her seat.

"Barbara is not leaving like I said earlier." Eunice gave a stern mommy-don't-play-that look to Titus. "You are clearly still grieving, or you would see what's good for you right in front of your face. There is nothing to discuss about my behavior when that woman showed she is not of God by striking me. Now we can talk, but it's going to be about you giving Barbara her job back and getting rid of Tisha." Eunice purposely mispronounced the girl's name. It was clear to her that Tosha was a fraud and probably wasn't even a real doctor. Who could finish medical school with a child? She thought it was laughable that her son fell for such a tale.

"Mother, you have no authority in who Kingdom Building Ministries employs. You have no authority in my personal life especially as it concerns my future wife and my daughter. As a matter of fact, you are being insubordinate now to your employer, and I don't take it kindly." Barbara stood up. She had known Titus long and well enough to know she and Eunice could get tossed out the church if they stayed on this path.

"Pastor Titus, I will leave out of respect for your mother. I wasn't there this morning, but the Titus I grew up with would never allow his mother to be disrespected or assaulted. He wouldn't tolerate such actions from anyone, but it's clear to me that *that* Titus is gone." Titus allowed Barbara's words to bounce off him like a rubber ball.

"Sister Barbara, you are correct. You were not there, and you don't know what you are speaking of, but thank you for excusing yourself." Barbara looked Titus in the eyes and saw nothing there. Eunice was right. He was lost in grief, and she had to be patient. She left without another word. When the door was closed, Titus addressed his mother.

"Mother, I apologize for Tosha slapping you, and she is willing to apologize to you as well when we return to my study."

"Are you crazy? I'm not going to be in the same room with her again."

"Mom, it's the Lord's day, and I have a sermon to minister. You know perfectly well you provoked her. You basically called an educated woman who gives herself to the community, tirelessly, trash. You called Summer an illegitimate child in front of her innocent face when you know nothing about her at all. If you had given me a moment to introduce you properly, you would have learned Summer's biological mother passed a little over a month ago—of breast cancer. Summer's mother's dying wish was for Tosha to take care of her daughter. We agreed to adopt and love Summer as our own." Eunice was speechless. She suddenly felt awful, but her stubbornness took over.

"That sounds like a wonderful fairytale, son, but that doesn't mean she is right for you. Now, I'm your mother, and Barbara Stoneheart is who God has for you. Honey, a mother knows. I knew it before Pearl, and you see what happened. The Lord wouldn't even bless you with a child. Now, you acting like Abraham and Sarah just gone do it yourself. Well, I won't stand by and watch that happen. That is why I am back." Titus stared at his mother and felt an overwhelming sadness.

"Mother, I can't keep you from feeling the way you do. Now, I see why Barbara had a delusion about there being something between her and me; you have been feeding her this stupidity. But you are mistaken, Mother, I'm a man of God, and I'm led by His Spirit and His will, not yours. If you can't accept my family, then I suggest you be prepared to be excluded. You are welcome to come back to my study, where Tosha will apologize for letting her anger take control. However—" Titus walked closer to his mother who had stood up during her rant.

"Mother, make no mistake about it. Tosha and Summer are my family. Today, I will be introducing Summer as my daughter and that my wedding date in six weeks. If you can't handle that or plan on causing a scene, please refrain from attending the worship service." Titus leaned in and kissed his mother on the cheek and said, "The choice is yours."

***

"Tosha! You did what?" Janine covered her mouth with both hands as she sat with her cousin and Tina listening to the horrors of the morning. They were sitting on the couch in Titus' office. Summer had Charity and Hope occupied with a hand-held gaming system. Deacon

Dewayne was giving Seth a tour of the church facility and grounds.

"I know, I was wrong, but that woman has an evil spirit. I think some of the demons she cast out overseas found a home in her."

"So, you were trying to lay hands on her?" Janine asked seriously not able to imagine her cousin, the doctor, hitting anyone.

"No, I was trying to slap her. I shouldn't have and, of all places, certainly not in the house of God and in the Pastor's study, but I couldn't help it." Tina knew something had taken place, but she too was stunned. She sat quietly and listened as she prayed for strongholds to be pulled down in the name of Jesus.

"So, what did Titus say to you?" Janine asked.

"He told me I was wrong and had to apologize. He said he was going to deal with her, but he understood that he should have let me leave before it escalated."

"Are you going to apologize?"

"Yes, I am. I have to. I was wrong, and that is not the example I should have set in front of Summer." Janine nodded, satisfied, and took her cousin's hand and reached for Tina's. She prayed a prayer of healing, forgiveness, and deliverance. When they were saying amen, Titus walked back through the door. Janine and Tina grabbed all three girls and scurried out of the office leaving the couple alone.

"How did it go?" Tosha asked in a whisper.

"Not well. My mother is disturbed, and there is nothing I can do about it at this moment." Titus sat next to Tosha and pulled her into his arms. She laid her head on his shoulder.

"I'm sorry, Titus. This is not how today was supposed to begin."

"Sweetheart, the enemy will always try to destroy happiness. We just have to crush him under our feet. Please don't apologize to me again. I forgive you, and we are going to get passed this."

"What about your mother? I need to say I'm sorry."

"Unfortunately, she is not ready to hear or accept it. We aren't going to let that deter us. Mistakes happen, mistakes are forgiven." Titus kissed Tosha on the top of her head.

"Now, we need to get our hearts and minds ready for service and make sure your family feels welcomed. We can only pray for my mother." Titus stood as did Tosha. At that moment, Deacon Dewayne knocked on the door alerting them it was time for the service. Titus and Tosha joined hands to enter the sanctuary of the Lord.

***

During the service, none of the parishioners had a clue what had happened earlier with the first family of KBM. In that holy place, the songs of worship lifted the downtrodden, and the anointing was breaking yokes. Tosha, standing with her cousin and best friend, repented again unto the Lord and received his forgiveness. She looked around the church for Mother Eunice. She wanted to say she was sorry, but she didn't see her, or Barbara, for that matter. She purposed in her heart to do it soon.

If the praise and worship didn't deliver a person out of whatever had them bound, surely the word from the Lord would. Pastor Titus preached a message titled, "What Will Separate You from the Love of Christ?" He dealt with matters of the heart that caused souls to go running to the altar, falling on their knees, while he spoke of not letting persecution, famine, sickness, death, or anything break the connection one has with Christ.

He told the people of God that their mistakes should not make them throw in the towel. If they fell, they should get back up again and finish the race. After he had closed his message, he had the minister of music sing Donnie

McClurkin's "We Fall Down." He laid hands on hundreds
of people, and many lives were dedicated to the Lord.

Afterward, he told his congregation about Olivia
Harvey and how Summer was now a member of the family.
Everyone in the building was on their feet clapping and
praising God for Summer. Titus motioned for her and
Tosha to join him. Summer proved she would be perfectly
fine in the spotlight. She took the microphone from her
Daddy Titus, and said, "Thank you all for letting Daddy
Titus and Momma Tosha keep me. My mommy in heaven
is happy, and I am too."

Just that quickly, all the trials of the day didn't
matter to either Titus or Tosha. The congregation was
ecstatic about their pending nuptials, and they were elated
to not only breathe again but to feel joy and love again.

Episode Thirty-One

"Eunice, all I'm saying is, I don't think this is grief
Titus is dealing with. I want it to be grief. But after
watching the service and hearing his message online today,
I think he is healed." Barbara shook her head in disbelief as
she sipped her coffee. She and Eunice were at her small
midtown home. Eunice believed her son was still mourning
Pearl, but Barbara had to admit to herself that even if that

were the case, Titus was not thinking about her. If she wanted a chance at happiness, she had to move on. However, Eunice was not trying to hear a concession speech from her prodigy. Eunice put her cup down and pointed her finger at Barbara as if Barbara was a child.

"Now you listen to me. I didn't cut my trip short, where I was doing the Lord's work, to come here and see you bow out like some flake. Titus is your man, and you have let one woman snatch him away from you, and I don't have any grandbabies yet. Now you stop giving yourself this self-pity party. Woman up! I tell you when Titus' daddy was alive and before we were married, I let him know I was the one for him." Eunice pointed her finger at her bosom and lifted her head like she appointed herself the queen of England.

"That's right, I sure did. He was liking me and another girl named Faith. Honey, I told her where she could get off and got my man. I was married for thirty years and was the best first lady until God called him home.

"For over a decade, I trained you to be the next first lady, but you keep letting other women take your man. Now, come on girl, we are not giving up. I've put too much time in you."

Barbara didn't know what to say or think. She just nodded. She was beginning to think Eunice was the one stuck in grief, and although she smiled at the old lady, Barbara knew in her heart that she needed a change.

***

At Momma Gladys' restaurant, the mood was festive as Pastor Titus and his family, the Owens, and Douglases shared in good southern cuisine. The three couples ate, laughed, and shared words of wisdom with one another. Their children played with electronics and had their own conversations led by Summer. Titus was especially impressed with Seth and Janine's story.

"You know, I read your book, *It Won't Prosper,* and was moved by your forgiveness, Janine, and your humbleness, Seth. However, hearing your testimony in person is just remarkable. I commend you both for sharing what you have been through with the world."

Janine nodded graciously accepting the compliment. Seth chose the moment to speak.

"It is only right for us to share this story. A life was lost because of my indulgence in lust and selfishness. If it weren't for the power of my praying wife, I could be lifting my eyes in Hell right now. But this lady prayed me through my sin and shame. She was light in the darkness of our marriage. When she could have easily let down her guards and walked away, she held up a standard and lifted Jesus up, and He saved me. So, I must tell everybody that He saves." The table went up with Hallelujahs and Amens. When Charity and Hope started saying "thank you, Jesus," and speaking in tongues, they all laughed. It was a great night to be a child of the Highest and a wonderful night to be in love and with family.

Episode Thirty-Two

Over the next few weeks, Tosha and Titus were busy balancing two households, spending time with Summer, and getting to know all there was to know about one another. Little things, like the fact that Tosha didn't like cheese on sandwiches, and Titus had a phobia about onions. They spent every waking hour they could with one another planning their wedding and bringing the Pearl Health Ministry Facility up to state code. Titus had to continue his duties as the Pastor of KBM, which included countless meetings, counseling, and worship services. He had declined all requests for him to officiate revivals in the city of Memphis and abroad. That decision had his mother, Eunice, as the head of Foreign Missions, calling a meeting to express her concerns.

"I understand the Pastor is getting married, but I see no reason why he can't do local revivals a night here and there. The payment he receives goes to the Missions Department, and that is how we help the widows, widowers, sick, and single parents." Eunice made her case to the Deacons and Trustees in the room as if Titus was not her son but some negligent Pastor forsaking his duties of the ministry. All heads turned to the Pastor. This was his mother calling him out, and they were not about to touch this.

Titus had no problem addressing his mother's concerns. "Sister Smith, I understand the missions' needs for funding, and I will personally donate five-thousand dollars to the foreign ministry. I'm doing that because you are correct; for over a year, I haven't been speaking outside of KBM. It started when I was in a bereaved state, and upon returning, my focus was in making our Health Ministry into a functioning clinic. Now as you all know, I'm weeks from marrying, and I have a daughter. These things are my priority and focus, now and moving forward." Titus took a drink of his bottled water as he watched his mother's face turn hard as stone, but he continued. "My calling is that of a pastor, not an evangelist. The Missions Department should not plan events or aid on income from my speaking engagements going forward. Because my priority outside of this ministry will be Tosha and Summer." Titus looked to his mother for acceptance, but she was anything but accepting. She waved off her son's remarks and turned to the other attendees in the meeting.

"What do you gentleman have to say? If the Pastor is cutting out an income stream to focus on his own agenda, how will the Missions Department efficiently be funded?"

Deacon Will Grant spoke. "Sister Smith, we can get with the financial secretary and have her look at the Missions Department's budget and see how we can accommodate. Pastor Smith is not contracted to accept any speaking invitations outside of KBM. He is free to accept or deny at his discretion. That is a clause in his employment contract. We understand your husband, the late Pastor Smith, funded the Foreign Missions Ministry that way, but Pastor Titus Smith is not bound by that tradition."

"Thank you, Deacon Grant. If there are any other matters to address?" Titus asked, and other topics were discussed and resolved. Eunice remained silent the rest of the meeting, but she was seething on the inside. She took out her phone and texted Titus and Tosha.

Eunice - I will not be attending your wedding and will make sure the Lord's people know why.

Titus – Mother, it will be wise of you to stop whatever scheme you are planning. Nothing you do will stop the Lord's will concerning my family. However, your employment at KBM is negotiable. You are welcome at my wedding and in my family, but that is your choice.

***

While Titus spent his morning in meetings, Tosha had a wonderful day wedding shopping with Tina and Janine. Titus had offered to pick up Summer, so they had the day to themselves. After the ladies had all found dresses, they headed to Tosha's house where they were treated to a full salon treatment by Dee Day, a mobile cosmetologist with a glam squad.

The ladies were passing pictures of Tosha's beautiful classic white gown around to Dee and her nail technicians. Tosha looked like a doll when she tried the dress on earlier in the day. The dress was regal and captured the radiance of Tosha's spirt. Tina and Janine couldn't have been happier with their full-length, one-sleeved, red gowns. With their tall, curvy frames, they looked like runway models. Janine was happy she had gotten off all the baby weight. Then there was the beautiful red and black princess dress for Summer.

"Oh, that is what's happening!" Dee exclaimed as she flat ironed Janine's curly locks to long, silky strands.

"I'm gonna hook y'all up that day, and my squad will have your nails, feet, and make-up on point. Now, let me see what the men are wearing." Tosha showed the traditional black groomsmen tuxedos with red vests and bow ties. When Dee saw a tuxedo modeled by Sean Combs himself, she stopped flat ironing and fanned herself. "Oh, I love P-Diddy almost as much as Usher. The Pastor gonna be fine in that white smoking jacket." Dee was a comedian, and she had the ladies and her staff laughing. Tosha had not felt this light and happy since she didn't know when. After they had calmed down, they began to chat.

"Tosha, when are Aunt Martha and Uncle Wade coming to town?" Janine asked her cousin. Uncle Wade was her father's brother.

"Mom and Dad are coming in a week earlier from Augusta, Georgia. We have FaceTime'd them countless times, but they are looking forward to meeting Titus and Summer."

"So, they're happy with everything?"

"Goodness, yes. Mom is acting like I'm marrying the President of the United States, and Daddy isn't much better."

"I think that is wonderful. I'm so happy for you, cousin." Janine said with misty eyes.

"Me too, and to think, I'm the reason for all of this." Tina caused the laughter to begin again.

"And I will forever be in your debt. That's why I have two matrons of honor—my best friend, and my best cousin." Tosha winked. She reached for her phone as she had a text alert. When she read the text from Eunice, she passed the phone to Tina, who passed it to Janine. Tosha knew she was too happy. All she could say was, "And the drama begins."

Episode Thirty-Three

Janine was the first to speak. "What drama? Your man has handled his mother in his text." Janine passed Tosha back her phone. "Don't let Mrs. Smith's threats ruin your mood and our great day. She is just trying to control her son. You two have done nothing wrong, so don't worry about it. Titus loves you and won't let anyone, not even his mother, destroy what you have." Janine gave her cousin a rub on her back. She was all too familiar with outside forces coming against marriages. She'd experienced much work within her own marriage, only, in Janine's case, her husband had fallen into temptation. She had remained steadfast in her faith, commitment to her relationship, and the Lord, and He had worked everything out in her marriage. She was confident that if He did it for her, He would do for Tosha. Tina walked over and wrapped her arms around Tosha's shoulders.

"Janine is right. She is speaking from experience. Don't let Mother Smith get to you. Dewayne and I have been married for years, and at first, his older sister couldn't stand me, but I continued to show her kindness even when that chic was being downright hateful. Did you know she invited Dewayne's ex-girlfriends to my bridal shower?" Tina observed both ladies looks of shock.

"Are you serious?" Janine asked with widened eyes. "His ex-girlfriend came to your bridal shower?"

"That's why I'm not having one," Tosha stated matter-of-factly.

"*Ex. Girlfriends.*" Tina clarified. "Three of them showed up on a mission with Asia. But you know what? I greeted them all with hugs and was nice as I could be. Did it bother me deep within? Yes. But after an hour, they all left. They couldn't take my kindness."

Tosha was encouraged by her friend's testimony and deleted the text message.

"Thank you, girls. I'm going to be like Taylor Swift and let 'the haters, hate, hate, hate' and 'I'm going to shake it off, shake it off.' " Tosha sang the lyrics while dancing like Carlton on the Fresh Prince of Bel Air. The ladies fell into laughter and continued to enjoy their day of leisure.

Episode Thirty-Four

Tosha was signing a stack of contracts from the city regarding Pearl's Health Facility. She had a dozen potential employees' ethics examinations to review before she could fully staff the facility. The endless paperwork was her least favorite task. She was reviewing one of the insurance contracts for the facility. The Legal Department had made notes for her to understand the legal jargon in the contract. For that, she was eternally grateful. Otherwise, she would miss picking up Summer due to all the "therefore" and "in lieu of" terminology that may as well been a foreign language to her. However, with their notes, she was making progress. Her attention was dragged away from the document when Tina Douglas, who was now her full-time executive assistant at the facility, buzzed in on her desk phone.

"Dr. Hightower, I'm sorry to disturb you, but I have Sister Barbara Stoneheart who wants to see you. She has assured me she is sincere in what she wants to discuss and is not here to make a negative scene." Tasha took off her reading glasses and thought, *what now?* She had no desire to deal with Barbara. She and Titus had recently worked through his mother's objection and threat of sabotage of their wedding plans. Now Barbara has something up her sleeve. Nonetheless, something deep inside her would not turn Barbara away. She pushed her talk button on the phone.

"Send her in."

Tosha put away the stack of contracts into her desk drawer. She stood up as Tina opened her door and entered with Barbara following. Without a word, Tina motioned with her hands for Barbara to take a seat in one the matching chairs across from Tosha's desk. She turned to her boss and friend giving her a look that said, *I got your back if this chic tries something.* Tosha, with amusement in her eyes, inwardly thought how fortunate it was to have Tina as a friend.

"Thank you, Sister Tina." Tosha gave her a wink letting her know she would be fine. Tina exited the office.

Seated behind her desk, Tosha clasped her hands together on her desk.

"Sister Barbara, what do I owe this pleasure?" Tosha gave a tight smile as she waited for a response. Barbara shifted in her seat displaying how uncomfortable she was. Tina waited with a raised eyebrow for Barbara to state her purpose.

"I don't want you to think that I'm here to threaten you or cause any more confusion. I'm here to say, I'm sorry and that I have my letter to submit to the church secretary that I'm leaving KBM. I've finally come to my senses and realize Titus is not in love with me, and I never had a chance." Barbara paused to wipe the tears from her eyes. Tosha grabbed a few Kleenex, which she took to Barbara, handing them to her. Tosha slid into the matching chair beside her.

"Barbara, thank you for telling me this, but are sure you want to leave KBM? Pastor Titus is concerned about your soul and your spiritual growth. I'm positive that has not changed." Barbara wiped her eyes and blew her nose while shaking her head in the affirmative.

"I'm sure, Tosha. It's time for me to let go and move on with my life. I allowed Mother Eunice to fill my head with fantasies that are just that, fairytales. It's not all her fault. I've wanted Titus for as long as I can remember. But the fact that he married Pearl should have been when I let go, but I served them both while coveting Titus all along. So yes, I'm sure. I will be joining Liberty

Fellowship and seeking therapy there. I just wanted to stop by and tell you I'm sorry and to watch out for Mother Eunice. I'm concerned for her sanity, and I know she is out to sabotage your wedding. I won't be participating in that. I am letting go of the crazy." With that, Barbara sat erect in her chair as a woman who had released a heavy burden. Tosha reached out her hand, and Barbara accepted the squeeze.

"Thank you for coming, Barbara, and I wish you well. I will be praying for you." Tosha stood prompting Barbara to rise.

"Come, I will walk you out." Tosha walked with Barbara, and they gave one another a quick hug. Barbara headed out of the suite of offices. When she was gone, Tina looked at Tosha.

"Well, what did she want?"

"She apologized and told me she was letting go and moving her membership to Liberty Fellowship."

"Seriously? Well, I better warn Pastor Caine what's coming his way." Tina said jokingly.

"Stop that. I believe she was sincere and forgive her. Life is too short to hold grudges. Now, let me get back to these contracts so that I can pick up Summer on time." Tosha went back to her office to work, praising the Lord for that battle being won. She would tell Titus this evening about the warning Barbara gave concerning his mother.

Episode Thirty-Five

"Daddy Titus, how many more days before we get married?" Summer asked as she used the dishcloth to dry the plate he had passed to her after rinsing it. They had finished dinner. Now, Titus was washing the dishes while Summer sat on the cabinet counter next to him. Titus smiled as he listened to his little girl tell him about her day in kindergarten and all that came to her inquisitive mind. As time passed, he loved her more and more.

"We have just two more weeks before I marry Momma Tosha." Titus took some of the soap suds and put them on her nose. Summer giggled and wiped her nose.

"Hey, I'm not a dish." Summer rubbed the suds off her nose and smiled up at her daddy.

"You're not? You sure about that? I see some areas behind your ears that need to be cleaned." Titus tickled Summer behind her ears then her neck.

She squealed, "Daddy, no!"

Titus stopped for a split second when he realized Summer didn't say Daddy Titus, but Daddy. His heart started beating rapidly against his chest. He never thought that title would make him feel ten feet tall but it did, and he was better for it. After Summer had stopped laughing, they finished up the dishes, and he walked her to the family room where Tosha was working on her laptop.

"Momma, Daddy tried to wash me like a dish." Summer ran to Tosha who barely had time to put her laptop to the side. Summer wrapped her arms around Tosha's neck, and Tosha kissed her cheek.

"He did, did he? What do you think about being a dish?"

Summer giggled. "I'm not a dish."

"No, you aren't, but you do have to get cleaned. Come on, let's go run your bath water, then Daddy Titus will read you a bedtime story." Tosha scooped up Summer while Titus took a seat on the couch and grabbed the remote. At the next words Summer uttered, Tosha froze mid-step as Titus let the remote drop.

"Mommy, since we are going to be a family, I'm just going to call Daddy—Daddy and you—Mommy."

"You are?"

"Yes, ma'am. That's what my real Mommy told me in my dream last night. Is it okay?" Summer asked while her big brown eyes widened.

"Of course, honey, me and uh . . . Daddy don't mind." Tosha swung around while holding her five-year-old daughter tightly on her hip. She locked eyes with Titus whose eyes were now liquid filled.

"Mommy is right, baby girl. We are honored to be called your mommy and daddy," Titus croaked out.

"Because we are family, and I can't wait for us to get married." Summer squealed.

Tosha made her way down the hall, hugging her precious daughter. Her day had been rough, and she still needed to talk to Titus about Barbara Stoneheart's visit.

However, Summer just made her day shine like a bright sunny day.

***

After Summer was bathed, had a story read to her by her dad, and was tucked in fast asleep, Tosha and Titus sat on the couch looking over the wedding plans.

"You are sure that everything is booked and you have everything you want?" Titus asked Tosha as she put her wedding binder on the living-room table. She sat back on the couch, and Titus moved over and pulled her into his arms to rest. He picked up one of her hands and laced his fingers with hers as he listened, waiting for her to speak.

"Yes, honey, everything is as I wish. Tina and Janine have made everything happen. The wedding planner you hired for me has just been running their errands."

"Good, that's what I want to hear. I want your day to be everything you have dreamed of." Tosha turned in his arms to look at him.

"Titus, it could be just you, me, and Summer, and that would make my dreams come true. I am blessed that you love me and want me to be your wife." She settled back in his arms as he kissed her on the top of her head.

"I'm the blessed one. After Pearl passed, I just knew that the Lord had taken the only girl meant for me away. I didn't question him. I just prayed for his grace to carry me through. The Lord answered my prayers and led me to revamp the Health Ministry, and he sent me you. Not only did he send me a girl that he had designed for me, but he sent us an angel. Sweetheart, the Lord gave me double for my trouble like His word said he would do. I'm blessed beyond measure, and I am happy to love again. Tosha Hightower, I am deeply in love with you." Tosha couldn't speak as she felt Titus lift their entwined hands and kissed hers tenderly. Tears that she could not fight flowed down her cheeks. She was in heaven on earth, and it was all because of this wonderful man, Titus Timothy Smith.

"I love you, and am in love with you, Titus. I'm going to do everything with the power of God so that I can be who you and Summer need me to be. I've never known love like this, and I will protect what we have with every fiber of my being." They sat for long moments as Titus absorbed the commitment his love had made to him. He couldn't remember a time when he was this happy and content. Sure, his mother was at war with him, and people were accusing him of rushing into marriage. But none of that mattered, he was happy, and nothing was going to ruin it.

"Babe," Tosha called out bringing Titus out of his thoughts.

"Yes, sweetheart."

"Barbara Stoneheart visited me today." Stunned, Titus patted Tosha on the back signaling she needed to sit up on her own.

"What did she want?"

"She wanted to let me know she was conceding in her chase for you. She told me she was going to join Liberty Fellowship Church. She also told me to watch out for Mother Eunice because she kept giving her hope that she had a future with you." Titus rubbed his hand over the locks of curls on his head. He was still getting adjusted to not having a shaven head and looked at Tosha.

"So, she left the church?"

Tosha thought to herself, *isn't that what I just told him? Is he hurt because she left the church? Is he going to go after her and bring her back to his fold?* "Yes, that's what she told me."

Tosha was now nervous that Barbara leaving the church would change their course. She waited, barely breathing, for Titus to stop rubbing his gorgeous hair. She loved every curl on his head but needed him to talk to her.

"Well, I hope she finds what she is looking for. Pastor Caine has an excellent ministry, and Dr. Whitney is a world-renowned therapist. She should be fine there, at least, I pray she is." Titus pulled Tosha back into his chest and turned. He grabbed the remote to turn up the volume for the evening news.

"So, you are okay with her leaving the church?" Tosha asked not wanting to hear the truth if it would mean Barbara had a special place in his heart.

"Yes, I'm fine with it. I want the best for everyone, and Barbara's attachment to me was unhealthy for her. I believe that my mother filled her with false hopes, but I'm dealing with mom." Tosha nodded her head in acceptance and made herself comfortable in Titus' arms and watched the evening news. It was full of depressing stories, but she was in good company.

Episode Thirty-Six

Barbara was awakened by her ring tone "Put a Praise on It," by Tasha Cobb. She reached her hands from under the cover to reach for the phone. The temperature outside was below freezing, and she wanted the least amount of her body exposed. With the phone under the cover, she didn't look at the screen to see who was calling.

"Hello."

"Barbara, tell me it's just a rumor. Tell me you are not leaving KBM." Barbara knew who was on the other line, but she pulled the phone from her ear to read the name on the screen. It was Mother Eunice.

"Eunice, it's not a rumor. I've decided to change membership." Barbara's tone was harder than she intended, but her voice was hoarse from just waking up.

"Why are you letting that woman run you away? What did she say when you were summoned to her office to cause you to give up on your man?" Barbara sat up in bed. It was clear this call would not be a quick one.

"Where did you get that I was summoned to anyone's office? You know what? Don't answer that because your source was wrong. I went to Dr. Hightower's office to apologize for the way I treated her, and to let her know, I was moving on, and she wouldn't have any more issues with me."

"Barbara Stoneheart, I never figured you were a quitter. I can't believe you are just going to bow out and let yet another woman claim your man." Barbara closed her eyes. She was still sleepy. She was also tired of this conversation.

"Eunice, I was never in the game to win Titus. He has never been in love with me or seen me more than anything else besides a dear friend. Now, that is over because I crossed the line trying to force what you and I wanted on him."

"Oh, Barbara, my son is just confused right now. He wants you. Now, you resend your separation notice to the church. We have time to stop this mistake of a marriage. I've already started putting things in place."

"Eunice, it's over! I'm done with that fantasy because that is all it ever was. I won't be returning to KBM. I'm moving on with my life. I have a new job at The Christian Bookstore on Third Avenue. I'm an associate manager and must be in by nine this morning. I have two more hours of sleep to get before it's time for me to get up. So, I'm ending this conversation. I love you Eunice and wish you would just let Titus be. You are only going to alienate him further if you don't."

"Don't tell me anything about the son that came out of my womb. He is grieving and about to make a huge mistake. And you, being the coward, have decided to let him make the biggest mistake of his life. Well, you hear me good, Barbara Stoneheart. That. Wedding. Will. Not. Come. To. Pass. You need to watch the evening news on Channel Twenty tonight at six. You'll regret you gave up on your destiny."

"Eunice, please don't go on the news talking against Titus. It's only going to leave you hurt." Barbara waited for a response, but when she didn't get one, she looked at her phone and saw the call had ended. She sighed and swung her legs out from underneath the covers. What could she do? She pulled up her text app and chose Titus' and Tosha's telephone numbers.

Barbara - GM. I just want to warn you both
that Eunice is planning to go on the six
o'clock news, channel 20, to speak against

your pending marriage. I'm not a part of it
and wish you two well. Barb. S.

Barbara returned her phone to the nightstand. Suddenly, feeling hot with anguish, she dropped down on her pillow, kicking all her covers to the side.

Episode Thirty-Seven

"We have Brother Seth and Sister Janine Owens to speak on the first Sunday of your honeymoon. The next Sunday, Associate Minister Lance Williams will speak."

Deacon Dewayne read, from his tablet, all the positions that were to be covered while the Pastor was on his honeymoon. Titus was going through his phone as he listened. On an average day, Titus received no less than three hundred text messages. They were becoming difficult to manage, but he read each one and responded to them all. He raised his hand for Dewayne to stop speaking. He wiped his eyes as he reread the text from Barbara. He quickly dialed Tosha's cell but didn't get an answer. He put his cell back on his hip holster. He then picked up his landline and dialed Tosha's office extension while Deacon Dewayne sat quietly observing his Pastor and friend's frantic behavior.

"Hello, Pastor Titus." Tosha cooed into the phone, letting Titus know she hadn't read the text message. Maybe she got as many as he did.

"Hi, Sweetheart, have you read a text from Barbara Stoneheart today?" Deacon Dewayne, looking up from his tablet, mouthed, *what is going on?*

"No, honey, I haven't had a chance to look at my phone all morning. I was late dropping Summer off this morning. We were headed to the car when I realized she hadn't brushed her teeth. We turned around to do that, just for her to squeeze the purple paste on her white shirt. So, I had to press another one and get her re-dressed." Tosha sighed while opening her desk drawer where her purse was. She fumbled in it until she felt her phone. "Needless to say, we were caught in rush hour traffic and were late. So, I haven't thought about my phone. I have it out now; let me check." Tosha scrolled through her message app stopping on a text of Charity and Hope riding the merry-go-round at the Wolfchase Mall. She sent a message back to Janine.

Too cute, we have to go back with Summer soon.

"Babe, have you seen the text?" Titus asked, which wiped Tosha's smile off her face.

"Oh, sorry. Janine sent me the cutest picture of the twins. I got sidetracked. I'm looking now . . . here it is." There was a long pregnant pause as Tosha read the text.

"Titus, what are you going to do? What could your mom possibly have to say on the news? How are you? Do you need me to come to your office?" Tosha rushed her many questions.

"No, sweetheart, I'm fine. I was just checking on you to make sure you were okay and that all this madness hasn't scared you away."

"Never. You got me forever, babe. Do you want me to respond to Barbara? I'd rather I deal with her versus you." Tosha really meant that. She also wasn't crazy with the fact that Barbara was just coming to terms with not having a future with Titus. No way was she sending her man into that web.

"That's fine, sweetheart. You can reach out to her. I have to figure out what my mother dearest is up to."

"Okay, honey, I have a couple of meetings I have to go to before I can go pick up Summer. Will you be coming over tonight?"

"It will probably be just to tuck in Summer. Be careful out there when you are driving. Love you!"

"Love you too, bye."

Tosha texted Barbara as soon as she hung up the phone with Titus.

Barbara, thanks for the information. Please reach out to me if you need to talk.

Tosha put the phone back in her purse and picked up her tablet to attend a series of meetings she had in the conference room.

Titus rubbed his hands across his head then down his face. Deacon Dewayne looked on with concern.

"Is everything alright, Pastor? What's going on with Mother Eunice and Sister Barbara? Well, I know Sister Barbara sent her notice of ceasing her membership here, but what else is going on?"

"Dewayne—" Titus lost formalities when speaking to Dewayne on personal and crucial matters. "It seems as though my mother will be on the evening news. I can only assume it will be against my leadership and pending nuptials." Titus got his cell phone off his hip and pulled up the text message from Barbara. He tossed the phone over his desk for Dewayne to catch, which he did with one hand. Dewayne read the text while shaking his head in disbelief. When he was done, he slid the phone back to Titus.

"It seems as though Sister Barbara is serious about moving on. But what are you going to do with your mom and the news? Do you want me to call up legal and ask if we can stop the segment from airing?" Titus shook his head in the negative.

"I don't think there is anything we can do about that." Titus opened his desk drawer and picked up the remote to the television mounted on his office wall. "Maybe we can catch the midday news and get a glimpse of what they will be airing this evening." Dewayne turned his chair around so he could view the news.

Though they thought they were going to get a glimpse of what the evening news would air, they were mistaken. Titus and Dewayne were dumbstruck when the first face that appeared on the screen was none other than Mother Eunice Smith.

"I am asking for the community to pray for my son, Pastor Titus Smith. He is grieving, and the grief he is suffering over the death of his beloved wife, Pearl, is great. He is marrying a woman he barely knows out of pure loneliness. This woman was brought to our church to help us honor my precious daughter-in-law's memory by serving those in our community who are faced with breast cancer. Instead of doing what she was hired to do, this woman has preyed on my son's vulnerabilities. Now he is making changes that will not only affect our local church but the community. Because of this gold digger, our Foreign Missions Department will no longer be able to aid the homeless, sick, and the less fortunate. I love my son, and he is a good man. He is just grieving. But I know if the citizens of our great county make a plea to him, the Lord will touch his heart, and we can continue the good work." The screen went back to the news anchor.

"You just saw the cry of a mother regarding her son, the well-known and respected Pastor Titus Smith. Tonight, at six, we will sit down with Mother Eunice Smith to speak in-depth on what has become of the once thriving Kingdom Building Ministries. On to other topics, . . ."

Titus and Dewayne couldn't make a move. They just sat there staring at the news with their mouths agape.

Episode Thirty-Eight

Titus hit the power button to turn off the television. He was livid. "Deacon Dewayne, please get H. R. to the main conference room, along with legal, the Missions' admin, and the Coordinator of Programs and Events. Their names have escaped me, but you know who they are. I'll be in there in half an hour."

"Yes, sir, I will have everyone there." Dewayne bustled out of the office to assemble everyone. He did not need to be told how urgent this matter was.

Titus dialed the only person he wanted to speak to.

"Hello, Son, I was expecting your call."

"I'm sure you were, Mother. You need to know you have crossed the point of no return. Expect your termination package by the end of the business day. Sister Eunice Smith, you are no longer the chair of the Kingdom Building Ministries. And, Mom, you are not to attend my wedding. I will have security make sure you can't step foot on the parking lot. Until you get the help you so desperately need, you are not welcome around my fiancée or child. I will be praying for you, Sister Eunice." Titus disconnected the call with his mother. He called Tosha and told her to head to the main conference room. He would fill her in face-to-face.

The next few hours were spent with Titus working with his staff to put out the fire his mother had started. The Legal Department contacted the news station manager. They advised the manager that if the station did an interview with anyone other than Pastor Titus or an authorized staff member of the Kingdom Building Ministries, they would be served with a lawsuit. In addition to that, legal informed them that the annual Christmas Parade that KBM partnered with them on would be the sole responsibility of the station and any other partners they had. KBM was out and would not be participating. Apparently, they had forgotten all that Pastor Titus, the CEO, did with the station for the city. Within the first hour, after that call was made, the interview was recanted, and a public apology was issued for the story airing prematurely.

Eunice's separation papers as an employee of the Kingdom Building Ministries Incorporated was sent by courier, as well as, paperwork informing her that her membership privileges were revoked. She was barred from all properties owned by the corporation and ministry. The last task Titus needed to accomplish was to ensure his family's safety. He and Tosha were on their way to the police station. They were both filing a restraining order against his mother. He hated to do it, but it had to be done. Tosha didn't think it needed to go to that level, but Titus had been so fervent in his instructions that she stayed quiet and did as she was asked.

By the time Tosha was on her way to pick up Summer, she was tired from the day. After she returned to the office from the police station, she was bombarded with calls from her parents, Tina, and Janine. She assured them all that she was fine and had to repeat the events of the day on each call. Her father expressed her need to marry Titus today. He was proud of how he handled the situation. Her mother wanted her to bring Summer to their home until the wedding, but Tosha didn't see a need for that. Titus had reassigned most of the security guards on staff to be her personal bodyguards. Again, she didn't think that was necessary but stayed quiet. Titus was not asking questions or taking comments today. He was the commander and chief, and she understood it. Therefore, by the time she picked up her energetic daughter, she had decided they were going through the drive-thru at McDonald's for dinner.

After dinner, Tosha helped Summer with her homework, watched a movie with her, helped her bathe, and tucked her in. True to his word, Titus came to read Summer her bedtime story. When Summer was asleep, he went to check on Tosha. She had been quiet most of the day. He prayed he hadn't frightened her. After he had time alone, he realized he didn't get her opinion on anything, and that was not how he wanted to start their union. But when he made it to the family room, she was fast asleep on the couch. She was in her pajamas, so she had showered while he spent time with Summer. He went over to the couch and picked her up. He carried her to the bedroom and put her underneath the covers. Titus gave her a kiss on the forehead and prayed over her that she had a sweet sleep. As he made his way out of Tosha's bedroom and out of her home, all he could think of was his mother and how he could help her from afar.

Episode Thirty-Nine

Titus was taking down pictures from his bedroom wall and clearing out closet space for his bride. When he realized he was in love with Tosha, he had stored the pictures of his life with Pearl in the attic. Titus had them professionally wrapped by a moving company. Now, he was taking all the décor down. He wanted Tosha to decorate and make this her home. He loved the eclectic style of her home and trusted her taste. He had made the offer of selling his home and buying a new one for them to share. However, when Tosha found out he had no mortgage, she said there was no sense in starting over. She was comfortable with the idea of living in his home. They had decided to use Tosha's house as a transition home for women who were in abusive relationships or recently released from prison. Tosha's commitment to the ministry was another reason he felt blessed beyond measures to have found her. He'd recently sent Sister Tina a one-thousand-dollar gift certificate to a local spa for recommending Tosha to head The Pearl Health Ministry. The vibration of his cell phone against his waist pulled Titus out of his thoughts. He took out the phone and saw it was his mother. He pushed talk and put the phone to his ear as he kept preparing his home for his family.

"Hello."

"Son, tell me it isn't so. A man of God would not put a restraining order on his own momma. I just know it had to be that woman! There is no way on God's green Earth you would do this to me!" Eunice yelled so loud Titus pulled his phone away from his ear and placed the call on speaker. He walked over to his couch and sat down.

"Mom, I did put a restraining order on you to stay away from Tosha and Summer for their safety. I did that because it is evident you have regressed back to some of your former ways."

"Titus, I was just speaking out as your mother, trying to protect you from making a big mistake. Now you have me banned from the church your father and I built from nothing, then I get served by the Sherriff's Department saying I have to stay away from my own son."

"Mother, please don't play games with me. You and I both know your history. Don't make me go down memory lane. You need help, and I am willing to cover your treatment and medication, if needed. But I will not sit on this phone listening to you lie."

Titus heard his mother gasp, but he didn't care. His mother had a problem. If she did not keep up with her antidepressants, pray, and read the word, she became unstable in her thoughts and actions. Today was all the proof he needed that she was spiraling down.

"I assure you, nothing is wrong with me, never has been. Everyone gets stressed sometimes. How long are you going to hold that over my head? My husband forgave me, and so did the Lord."

"Mom, my father enabled your insanity by constantly covering up your faults. How many young ladies did you threaten to stay away from me in high school by prophesying the wrath of God to them if they didn't heed your warning? What about Sister Sandra who merely sent Daddy a thank-you card for being there for her when she lost her husband? Mom, Dad paid that woman off not to press charges against you after you attacked her. I hate to go there with you, Momma, but that lady on the news today was the same lady who did that and so much more. So, hear me and hear me well, I gave the police and the staff at KBM the facts about everything. I am not Dad. I will not tolerate a wolf in sheep's clothing. Now, you can enter treatment and I will personally cover the cost, or you can live your life however you choose—if that is deceiving your own self then go ahead and do that. But, you will not have the opportunity to hurt my Tosha or Summer, not now, not ever." Titus waited for a response that never came. Eunice had disconnected the call, and he knelt on his living room floor and prayed for his mother.

Episode Forty

Eunice sat at her kitchen table drinking beer out of her crystal wineglass. She told herself it was just to calm her nerves this time. She had to process the disrespect her only child had dished out to her. He had all but cast her out of his life because of her love for him.

Who did he think he was, bringing up those misunderstandings from the past? If only her Beloved were still here, she wouldn't have to put up with this exile crap. Eunice picked up the picture of her deceased husband and traced the outline of his face. She kissed the portrait and placed it back on the table. She began to talk to the picture.

"How could he put a restraining order on me? Has he forgotten that his little doctor attacked me in his office?"

"No, No, I was only joking about the little girl and the doctor being a gold digger." Eunice sipped on her drink while she heard her belated husband speak. She loved when his spirit would come and comfort her.

She wiped at the tears streaming down her face. "I knew you would understand. If only you were here, I'd be the first lady and wouldn't have to worry about anything. Certainly, not this exile crap. You would make Titus see the error in his ways. You would never make me go back to a mental institution when I'm perfectly fine; our son is the one with grief and making poor decisions. But you go on back to resting now Beloved. I'll be okay." Eunice poured more beer into her glass and began to pray about her next move. After long moments of silent prayer and drinking, she had a new vision.

If Titus wanted to play her like this, fine. He could marry the wrong woman again and watch that family be destroyed too. She knew she was a woman of God and heard from the Lord. He didn't listen the last time, and it cost Pearl her life. Barbara was meant for him, but now that the will of God had changed because she too was now walking in disobedience. She'll see their lives crumble soon enough because God don't like ugly.

She would focus on people who cared about what the Lord wanted, she was a prophetess of The Most High God, and those who didn't heed her warnings would be damned, *thus said the Lord.*

Eunice sat back and thought to herself. *I'll start my own church to get the money coming back in. I can do this without my Titus. I'm sure people will follow me; I am their pastor's mother, and to most, I'm still the first lady of KBM. I'll send out a few texts and watch the tithes roll in.*

She drank the remainder of her beer down in one gulp. She picked up her phone and placed a call.

"Hello."

"Hey, girl, this is Eunice. The Lord just told me to start a new church. Can I count on you to be my first member?"

"You know it."

Eunice smiled a devious smile into the phone. "Great, I knew I could count on you. Welcome to the True Word Tabernacle, where your pastor is Mother Eunice Smith."

Act·Six

Episode Forty-One

Over a week later, the last thing on Tosha's mind was Eunice and Barbara. She was all about becoming the new Mrs. Titus Timothy Smith. Today was her wedding day, and no devil in Hell would ruin her mood. She was in one of the sitting rooms attached to the women's restroom. The room had been converted into a spa area for the bride and her wedding party. Tosha sat in the bride's glam chair as a cosmetologist worked on her hair, a make-up artist applied her makeup, and a manicurist polished her fingernails. As they worked, her thoughts were consumed by the last year of her life and how mysterious the way the Lord's works were. She recalled how Tina insisted she interview for the new health facility at KBM, and never in a million years did she think that interview would lead to more than a career opportunity. Oh, how she loved Jesus, he'd given her more than she could've asked or dreamed for. Today, she would marry the first man she had truly given her heart to. He was worthy of owning it. Titus had shown her through every situation that he would love, protect, and give her the world if she desired it. She was blessed to have this man who would shake up the city to secure her safety, and deny his flesh and blood if they stood against their family. The average man would have said no, but Titus welcomed Summer into his life and heart just as she had. He had proven time and time again that he would never forsake her.

"No tears now, beautiful. You are ruining this gorgeous face." Missy, the makeup artist, said as she grabbed Kleenex from her work station.

"I'm sorry." Tosha sobbed as her mother, along with Tina and Janine, came into the room.

"Tosha, what's wrong?" Her mother, Mary Hightower, rushed to her and knelt looking up at Tosha's tear-stained face. Mary grabbed the hand the manicurist wasn't working on.

"I'm sorry. I was just thinking of how blessed I was and got a little emotional." She pulled her hand from her mother and Lisa, the manicurist, and fanned herself. She had become warm with all the people surrounding her as her emotions overwhelmed her.

"Tosha, you are blessed, but you do not want puffy eyes in your wedding photos," Tina said sternly. "So, no more tears. And you must look flawless for Pastor and the photographer." Tosha nodded in agreement causing Dee Day to have to stop her progress on Tosha's hair.

"Now, Dr. Hightower, soon-to-be Dr. Smith, let's get it together. It is time to be fierce. We can all cry after the reception." The room fell into laughter as each lady looked on watching as Tosha was transformed into the most beautiful bride they'd ever seen.

When the room had cleared out, Tosha stood alone in front of the mirror loving what she saw. She pulled her veil to cover her face and said, "Goodbye, Tosha Dunson Hightower. I love you as you are, and I say yes to the will of God for my life as Tosha Dunson Smith." She turned from the mirror and walked out of the lounge and into her future.

Episode Forty-Two

The sanctuary had been transformed into a beautiful garden. There were at least one-hundred dozen roses used in the décor, forming bouquets around the stage. Each bouquet was strategically placed around the edge to give the appearance of roses sprouting from the floor, as they would in an outdoor garden. There was green flooring that added the grass element and in the center of the stage was a canopy where the couple would exchange their vows, draped with black silk. The view from any angle in the church was breathtaking.

Every column in the sanctuary had rose vines wrapped from top to bottom. The lighting had been dimmed from the standard white, while twinkling spotlights rotated throughout the room. The atmosphere was one of elegance and romance.

The ceremony was set to begin at two o'clock in the afternoon. Guests were ushered in an hour before as they arrived in their elegant black and red formal wear. The members of KBM, and friends and family of the bride and groom were dressed as though it were a presidential inauguration. Upon arrival, as they were photographed in the foyer, they were given a program and a token of love for attending. Each guest was then escorted by either male ushers or female hostesses down the red carpet that led to their seats. All in attendance knew this wedding would rival any put on by the British Royal family.

At the top of the hour, the side doors were closed. Any guest who was not already seated would have to wait until after the ceremony. Pastor Titus T. Smith walked in behind Pastor Derrick Caine, followed by Deacon Dewayne. Titus took in the beauty of the sanctuary and what Tosha had planned as their wedding scene. It was beautiful, and like nothing, he had seen before. That was saying a lot because he had officiated hundreds of nuptials.

Titus smiled as Babyface's "Our Love" played through the speakers. He watched the ushers come in and light the candles in the sanctuary. He took in the lyrics of the song and found them fitting. Their love *was* resilient. It had already stood through fires and the rain. Even though watching Mrs. Hightower being escorted down the aisle was bittersweet because his own mother was missing, he knew their love was worth every sacrifice. After the seating of the bride's parents and their honorary guests who were church officials, a member of the praise and worship ministry, Sister Cortrina, sang the Lord's Prayer. Finally, it was time for the wedding processional. The artists who would sing the song walked out and took their positions. The guests rose to their feet and applauded as K-Ci and JoJo began to sing the smooth lyrics of "This Very Moment." Titus nodded to his friends that he'd known for years and had counseled from time to time.

Titus had to close his eyes to fight back the tears. This day, this very moment—he never dreamed would come. But God had given him another chance to *love again.* This was certainly a day he had prayed to be beautiful for his bride and to know that this moment was meant for him and her. He took in the beauty of Janine being escorted by her husband, Seth, followed by Tina who walked alone because her husband was his right-hand man.

When his precious Summer, in her black and red silk dress, walked down the aisle dropping rose petals, the tears flowed from him like a river. She smiled the entire way. He almost came undone when she made it to the podium and ran up the stairs and across the stage, jumping into his arms. This brought laughter from the audience and joy from his heart. Janine and Tina both motioned for Summer to come to them, but Titus wouldn't have it. He held his daughter as a trumpet was played, and the doors swung open. In walked his beautiful bride escorted by her father as the world-renowned artists Ron Kenoly and Darlene Zschech sang "You Are." Titus beheld his beautiful bride and knew he was now with the final love of his life. This was an everlasting love, a second chance for him to love and hope. He would cherish this woman forever. Although the road that led him here was filled with some dark alleys, he wouldn't change this for any riches in the world.

As Tosha took each step into the sanctuary, she nearly broke down, especially when she saw Titus holding Summer. Her father, Steve, had to nudge her on. This man was her everything. She could not live without him because she had not truly been alive before him. Who else could love her so completely and accept their daughter without hesitation? In him, she was complete and found true happiness. When her father helped her up the stairs and finally placed her hand in Titus', she was filled with unspeakable joy. Tosha wasn't alone because Summer, with watery eyes, reached her little arm around her mommy and pulled the three of them into a group hug. The bridal party and all the guests were now in tears; some cries were audible. It took the professional Pastor Caine to call the ceremony to order and marry this couple ordained by God. Marrying Titus and Tosha gave Pastor Derrick Caine hope that love could happen again for him as well. His wife had recently left him for another woman. But the anointed love this couple shared through their vows and their passionate kiss, let Derrick know love wasn't over for him either. He was proud to do the honor of saying, "Ladies and Gentlemen, I present to you Pastor Titus and Dr. Tosha Smith with their daughter Summer Harvey-Smith."

Tosha looked at her husband with wide eyes. She had no idea the adoption would be final this soon, but the wink Titus gave her let her know he had accomplished the impossible.

The rest of the afternoon, the couple were hand in hand as they greeted their guests, took their first dance, made their toast, and listened to the roasts from their bridal party. It was a perfect day—right down to them smashing cake in one another's faces. That day that they gave their lives to one another was the day it was on Earth as it was in Heaven for them both. Titus and Tosha were looking forward to their life together. But first, they would enjoy a two-week honeymoon in Paris, France.

Episode Forty-Three

"Why can't I go to Paris? We family, and I'm a Smith too," Summer whined as Titus and Tosha were saying goodbye to her. It tore at both their hearts, but they had decided that Summer would stay with Cousin Janine, Cousin Seth, and the twins. Titus picked her up as she cried and mumbled out her fears. "What if you and Mommy don't come back? Then I won't have anyone again. Pleasssse, don't leave me." Titus had a mind to tell Tosha they were taking Summer with them, but Tosha stepped up and rubbed their little girl on the back and whispered soothing words to her.

"Summer, I promise we are coming back. You don't have to worry. Besides, you love to play with Charity and Hope. Cousin Janine said she would take you over to Mrs. Paige's house where you can play with her niece, Nikki, and the baby, Moriah. Doesn't that sound like fun?"

Summer loved to play with Nikki. They had gone to the same preschool. The thought of visiting her and baby Moriah made staying behind seem a lot better. She raised her head and nodded.

"Yes, ma'am, I love to play with the baby. Are you and Daddy going to make one so I can have my own baby sister or brother?" Just that quickly, her cries were gone, and a new request caused a lump in Tosha's throat.

"We will see what we can do about a baby Smith, but I promise you, we will bring you back lots of toys and books," Titus said while tickling her side. Summer squealed with delight. "Now, come on, baby girl, let's say goodnight to your cousins, and Daddy will read you a bedtime story."

"Yes, sir, but who's going to read me a story when you are away?" Summer asked.

"Baby girl, I will FaceTime you every night and read you whatever story you want to hear." Titus kissed her on the forehead as he placed her in a twin bed in the twin's bedroom. Charity and Hope slept in the same bed, not able to separate from one another even in slumber.

When Summer was asleep, Tosha and Titus thanked their cousins for all their help, and then they were off to the airport.

***

Tosha knew they were going to France, but what she didn't expect was to fly out of the private airport in Olive Branch, Mississippi, a city just south of Memphis, TN.

When the driver of their limousine opened the door for them, Titus got out first then turned to assist her. He pulled her into his body and kissed her where they stood under the moonlight. When the kiss ended, they were forehead to forehead, brown eyes gazing into brown eyes.

"Honey, this has been the best day of my life, thank you."

"I'm happy your day was what you wanted. Tosha, I plan to make our lives everything you want."

"You're already doing that." Tosha nodded her head toward the private plane where the driver and airport attendant were loading their luggage. "I just knew we were flying commercial. How did you pull this off without me knowing?"

"I have my ways." Titus teased, and Tosha frowned.

"No, seriously, it's a wedding gift from one of the couples from KBM. Brother Kenneth Alexander and his wife, Kimberly, came to me a few Sundays ago, offering their private plane and covering the next two weeks—where I plan to make sure your body knows what your mind and heart are aware of."

"And what's that?" Tosha felt her face and ears become warm.

"That." Titus kissed her forehead. "It." He kissed her temple. "Belongs." He kissed her on the nose. "To." He kissed her on the lips. "Me."

Titus scooped up his bride and carried her across the tarmac and up the stairs into the aircraft where they began their journey.

Episode Forty-Four

The private jet was luxurious with the latest technology, including a LCD television with satellite reception. There was a work area equipped with a conference table for meetings. The seats were leather, and there was enough space to stretch out. The three-person crew, comprised of the captains, and flight attendant, had set a romantic tone with chilled sparkling beverages, a buffet of finger sandwiches, cheeses, and fruit. Titus and Tosha did not have time to take in the opulence of the aircraft. The groom could not further delay quenching his physical need of his bride. They would have to enjoy the splendor of the cabin later. After they had been greeted by the crew, with Tosha still in his arms, Titus made his way to the bedroom. It was in that room that he took his wife for the first time, only to learn that she had kept her virtue until that very night.

"Tosha, baby, why didn't you tell me?" Titus asked as he held her in his arms after they had shared the most tender lovemaking experience he had ever taken pleasure in.

"You never asked. It's not like we talked about sex much. We agreed to wait until marriage because it was the Lord's will. I saw no reason to bring up the fact that I'd never made love before." Tosha said bashfully and buried her face against his shoulder.

"No, don't do that, love. There is nothing to be ashamed about. I am honored that you saved yourself for me, and I promise you will never regret joining your life with mine. With all that I am and with all that I have, I will make you the happiest you've ever been." With that declaration, Tosha grabbed her husband's face and kissed him as if her life depended on his taste. The two of them joined as one, husband and wife. They never got an opportunity to roam about the plane. They stayed entwined with one another the entire flight. They were truly on cloud nine.

Tosha could not think of a better honeymoon destination than Paris, "The City of Love!" She enjoyed every day, sightseeing with her husband. They went to every iconic monument, like the Eiffel Tower, the Louvre Museum and Notre Dame Cathedral. Their days were long and nights were endless as she cherished every moment with Titus. He never seemed to stop amazing her, like when she learned that he was fluent in French. She was a conversationalist in Spanish but enjoyed listening to him parler français with the locals.

The two weeks went by fast for Tosha, but she basked in the fact that he was hers and she was his for the rest of their lives. God was good, and life as Mrs. Titus T. Smith was great.

Episode Forty-Five

"Momma! Daddy! You're back!" Summer squealed as she ran out the Owens' front door. She had been standing in front of the window since her Aunt Janine said her parents were on the way. She flew down the stairs as fast as her little feet could carry her. She was met with arms wide open from her dad.

"Hi, princess, we missed you so much." Titus hugged her tight as he kissed her cheeks. "Did you miss Mommy and me?"

"Yes, sir, I did, but I knew you'd be back." Summer reached out her arms for her mom. Titus helped Tosha balance her. Summer was really too big for her mom to carry her, but Tosha made it work until they entered the house.

"Welcome home." Janine greeted Tosha and Titus with a hug. Seth came out of the family room to greet the couple holding Charity, with Hope following close behind.

"Hello, Pastor and Mrs. Smith, don't you two look lovely." Seth put Charity down to hug Tosha and shake Titus' hand. Charity went to her mother with her arms up. She was the three-year-old twin who had to be held and pampered, whereas Hope would kick and scream if someone tried to pick her up. Janine picked up her baby girl and ushered everyone into the family room.

"Come on, let's have a seat. You all aren't rushing off, are you? We want to hear about Paris." Janine inquired with a French accent.

"No, we are in no rush. We appreciate you keeping Summer for us." Tosha said as she sat on the couch, and Summer climbed in her lap. It wasn't until she saw her beautiful little girl did she realize how much she missed her.

"It was our pleasure. Summer helped me with the girls. She was my special helper. I haven't written so many chapters since I had them. Summer kept them entertained. She even got Charity to play for hours."

"You just have to give her something soft to play with, like a teddy bear or blanket, that's all." Summer said matter-of-factly as if she were a Red Cross certified babysitter.

"I'm proud of you for helping Auntie Janine," Tosha said as she hugged Summer. "Because you were such a big girl, we have presents for you." Summer's eyes were now huge as she thought about the new things she would have. "In fact, we have a little something for everyone."

"Oh, yay! You have something for Charity and hope too?"

"I sure do. Let me go to the car and get the surprises." Tosha placed Summer on her feet and started to get up. This movement caught Titus's attention as he was having a sidebar conversation with Seth.

"Babe, I will go get the bags. You stay here." Titus got up, and Seth followed.

"So, tell me, Tosha, how was the first time for you?" Janine asked blushing herself. She knew her cousin had waited until marriage. By the smile on Tosha's face, she could tell it was worth the wait.

"It was beautiful, everything about it, everything about him. I am so fortunate to have a passionate husband."

"Well, I am happy for you. You are the only other woman I know besides myself that did it the right way. You won't regret it, I promise. I'm so proud of you."

"Thanks, Janine. It was perfect. I couldn't ask for a better honeymoon."

"Did you all hear from Mrs. Eunice?" Janine took a deep breath.

"No, I haven't, and Titus hasn't brought her up, so I just leave the situation to him. Although I didn't miss the security we have here, per Titus it's for our safety." Janine reached out and rubbed her cousin's back.

"Has he told you why he felt the restraining order was necessary?" Tosha shook her head in the negative.

"No, he said we would discuss it all after the honeymoon. I wasn't trying to ruin our wedding or honeymoon discussing my mother-in-law."

"I don't blame you. It will all work out for the good, just keep believing."

***

Outside of the Owens' home, Titus and Seth were unloading the car with the gifts for the family when a man walked up into the driveway. Titus' security moved to stop him. However, Titus saw the gentlemen out of his peripheral and nodded to the security not to obstruct him. There was something familiar about him. Seth didn't recognize him but waited to see what he wanted.

"Excuse me, Pastor Titus," the man said nervously. "I was hoping I could speak to you for a moment." Titus looked at the man with a piercing glare.

"How did you know I would be here?"

"I knew you had to come back here. Your, umm, your daughter is here. I was at your wedding and saw her and knew she was staying here." The man pointed at the

Owens' home. Both Titus and Seth were now on guard, and Titus signaled with his hands for security to come closer.

"What is your name, sir?"

"I'm Brian Jackson." He extended his hand to Titus then Seth who both gave a handshake. Brian's eyes darted to the security closing in on him.

"I know it seems strange," Brian said with his hands up in the air in surrender. "But I've been trying to find my little girl, Summer. At least, there is a chance she may be mine. I had a brief affair with Olivia Harvey before I joined the military. I have been away for almost six years. When I returned, my mom told me Olivia had passed and had a little girl. My mom didn't know Olivia and I had anything going on before I left. If she had, she would have been there for my child. Olivia lived two doors down from my mom. Our affair was brief and not serious, but if that little girl is mine, I need to know."

Episode Forty-Six

Tosha could not believe this was happening to her. Just when all was well, just when she had the family she always wanted, Brian Jackson showed up and threatened to ruin everything. Tosha was in the shower allowing her tears to mix in with the body wash and hot water that sprayed down her body. Her cry was silent, but inside, her heart contained a thunder that caused a roaring in her ears. *This simply couldn't be.* "Lord, let it not be so!" she wailed and backed up in the shower with her hands in the prayer position as she looked toward heaven. "Lord please . . ." was all Tosha could get out before she slid down the shower's wall in despair. Her silent tears became audible as she cried out, "Jesus, help me!" She sat on the shower floor with her knees pulled into her chest and wept.

Titus was entering their master suite after reading Summer her bedtime story. It was bittersweet. All the months when he would read to her then go to his own home leaving her and Tosha behind were over. They were now in the home that belonged to all of them. However, if Brian Jackson was Summer's biological father, it could reverse the judge's decision for the adoption. Titus stopped then continued walking softly. As he walked further into the bedroom, he heard moaning coming from the bathroom. His heart dropped through his shoes when Titus realized that sound was his wife. He hurried to the restroom and swung the doors open. When he took in his wife sitting on the floor of the shower, he sprinted to close the distance between them. He opened the shower door and knelt to pick up his wife. She circled her arms around his neck and continued to cry. Titus used one hand to get a towel and dry her off. He took her into the bedroom where he dried his wife, applied lotion, and helped her into her gown. He pulled the covers back and tucked her into bed. Tosha allowed him to comfort her. She had no words to say; they were caught in her throat.

That's the beauty of being one with your love, she thought. *They know what you need when you need it.* Titus didn't need Tosha to express how she felt verbally. He could feel it in his soul. As he caressed her on the back, he whispered assurances to her.

"Sweetheart, I know you are afraid, but the Lord won't put anything on us that we can't bear. I believe in my heart that we won't lose her, but if that happens, we have each other. Brian said he wouldn't keep us away from her. Honey, you have me to hold you and comfort you no matter what, and our Father in heaven is holding us both. We will get through this."

Tosha heard the words and received them. She fell asleep, and it was a sweet one, despite all that was left up in the air for their family.

Episode Forty-Seven

Eunice was having a morning drink and watching a movie when her phone buzzed. She smiled at the picture on her screen. She had been expecting this call sooner.

"Did they believe you?"

"What, honey? I don't get a hello, or how are you doing?"

"Don't play with me. Tell me, did you do what I said? How did it go?"

"They listened to my story and agreed to a paternity test."

"Great, that buys us some time for you to go to the media and tell your story."

"Eunice, I don't think I should do that. They really love Summer, and she is going to be your granddaughter. When the paternity results show I'm not the father, they will go on being happy. And where will that leave you?" Brian was feeling guilty for allowing her to talk him into this crazy plan. But there wasn't much he wouldn't do to maintain the lifestyle that he had grown accustomed to.

"Brian, you let me worry about that and just keep doing what I pay you to do."

"Love, I'm just saying, all the moves you are making are only going to alienate your son, who is not this bereaved man you think he is. I saw him with his wife and daughter. They are in love, and that little girl loves them. I love you, and I wanted to meet my future stepson as your man, not a pawn in a chess game that you have no chance of winning." Eunice rolled her eyes. Brian could never just stay on task. What was with this generation—first Barbara, now Brian.

"You know there is no chance of us being romantically together in public. You are my assistant and a member of my congregation."

"Eunice, I am the only member," Brian interjected.

"That is all you will ever be. Now, if you want to keep wearing that fine clothing, living rent free in that nice house, and driving that new Range Rover I purchased for you, you will do what I say when I say it. No more foolishness about us getting married. I can't be a cougar. I am the wife of a respected pastor and a pillar of this community."

"You *were* the wife, Eunice. Seriously, I am beginning to think you don't know he's gone. I'm not going to the media and don't threaten me. I more than earn everything I have. Threaten me again, and the only place I'm going is to tell Pastor Smith I lied—and that you and I have been carrying on an affair for years—even before your dearly departed husband passed away. I will also tell him we were living it up in the Caribbean when he thought you were on a mission trip. A trip that was funded by his church." Brian was now up and pacing back and forth in his apartment. He no longer wanted to be a part of this scheme. He was waiting for her to come back at him. When she didn't, he called out to her.

"Eunice!"

She was there, but a pain was now shooting up her left arm, paralyzing it. Her heart was beating fast, and sweat was running down her brow. She could only murmur, "Help." It came out as a soft whisper.

"Baby, hold on! I'm calling 911." Brian disconnected and placed an emergency call giving Eunice's address. He grabbed the keys to his Rover and texted Pastor Titus.

> *Pastor Titus, please meet me at 8384 Strong*
> *Drive, 9-1-1.*

Episode Forty-Eight

Titus was reviewing resumes for KBM's open positions, one being his mother's. He felt a vibration against his hip alerting him of a text message. He pulled out his phone and read the text. He sat, bewildered for a moment because Summer's possible father texted him 9-1-1 and to meet him at his mother's house. He got up and grabbed his suit jacket, heading out of his office. He stopped to let Deacon Dewayne view the text.

"Deacon, look at this text from Brian Jackson."

Dewayne took the phone from Titus asking, "The guy claiming to be Summer's father?"

"Yes, one and the same." Titus watched Dewayne read the text with a frown on his face.

"You need me to go with you?"

"Yes, and get a security guard to go with us. I'm going to let Tosha know about this before we head out. I'll meet you in the parking lot."

"Yes, sir, we'll be out there."

***

Working always took Tosha's mind off her worries. Taking Summer to the DNA Testing Center was one of the hardest things for her to do. Summer was such a sweetheart by not asking questions about having to go to the doctor, which was rare. Summer usually had a "why" discussion about simply going to the grocery store. However, the Lord truly knew that she could not bear a ton of questions from her little girl this morning, and Summer stayed focused on her electronic game for most of the time.

Tosha was now in her office signing off on the last new hires for Pearl's Health Center and had a meeting with an event planner for the grand opening. The interior designer's staff was out in the foyer hanging the last portraits she had selected. Therefore, she didn't have time to focus on the looming test results that would seal the fate of her family. Tosha was brought out of her thoughts when there was a knock on her door. She looked up and saw Justice Johnston, an employee of Rachel's Interior Design.

"Excuse me, Dr. Hightower, I mean, Dr. Smith. We are finished in the foyer and would like you to take a look." Tosha smiled as she stood to follow Justice.

"I can't wait to see it. Please, lead the way." Tosha walked with Justice and enjoyed small talk as they went. Justice was a beautiful shade of honey. She bore a striking resemblance to the actress, Essence Atkins. Her height, big almond eyes, and even the shape of her mouth were the spitting image of the actress'. Justice was professional when in Tosha's presence; though, she had noticed Justice flirt with some of the male employees. Tosha hadn't said anything because she knew Justice's stint here was temporary and because the young lady had an awesome eye for detail. As they turned the corner entering the foyer, Tosha stood still as she saw her husband mesmerized by the photos on the wall. He and Deacon Dewayne were staring so intensely that she didn't know if it was good or bad. She thought to herself that there was only one way to find out. She took a deep breath and walked over to stand by Titus as Justice stayed back, obviously catching on to the tense vibe.

"Hi, honey, and Deacon Dewayne, what brings you to this side of the building?" Tosha gave a tight smile, feeling awkward as Titus turned to look at her.

"How and when did you get these pictures of Pearl?" Titus pointed to the various collages of Pearl that hung on the walls. There was a picture of her in various aspects of ministry. One portrait was of Pearl with the children of St. Jude's Hospital. She was reading a story. There was a picture of her helping senior citizens shop for groceries, and there were several other beautiful pictures that captured the legacy of Pearl Smith.

"I got them from the ministry leaders. I hope it's okay." Tosha swallowed feeling like she had made a huge error in judgment. "This is Pearl's Health Ministry, so I felt it was fitting to allow her works to be honored and for every patient to know this facility's inspiration." Titus stopped fighting the tears he was holding back and hugged his wife.

"Thank you, Tosha. This is a wonderful tribute to Pearl. Thank you for honoring her this way. It is more than okay. You are more than wonderful." Tosha sighed with relief as she embraced Titus. She was happy that he approved and hoped that Pearl was at peace when she looked down from heaven. She was not threatened by Pearl's memory. She would help her love remember the good because she was certain the best was yet to come. Dewayne and Justice looked on in awe at the beautiful couple.

Finally, Titus pulled away.

"Again, thank you, honey. I was taken by surprise when I saw the portraits. It made me forget why I came. I got a text from Brian Jackson to meet him at my mother's house. I wanted to let you know that Deacon Dewayne and I are headed over there with security." Tosha couldn't believe her ears.

"Why on Earth would he be with your mother? Do you want me to come?" Titus through his hands up while shaking his head.

"No, I just wanted you to know. I will call you when we get there, and I know what's going on." Titus leaned in and kissed her on the lips. "Don't worry."

He looked around at the foyer's décor. "Thank you again for this. You are amazing." Tosha smiled and waved him off. After he and Dewayne had left, she turned and smiled at Justice.

"Job well done!"

Episode Forty-Nine

Titus was filled with warring emotions as he sat in the back of his town car being driven by security. Dewayne sat in the front, stating Titus needed this time to clear his mind. Dewayne was correct. As he stared out of the window, taking in the beautiful fall landscape of Memphis, he was a man that couldn't keep up with his thoughts. There were so many fleeting images that entered his mind and vanished as quickly as they came.

First, he couldn't come up with a logical reason why Brian Jackson would be summoning him to his mother's home. Could Brian and his mother know each other, and were they plotting against him to steal his daughter? He quickly released that thought. There was no way his mother knew Summer's possible father.

That thought caused a squeezing sensation in his chest. The tightness in his chest almost took his breath away. He inhaled and exhaled deeply, trying to shake away the thought of losing his daughter. Titus struggled with the concept of no longer having Summer. He knew that it would destroy his wife. He prayed that it wouldn't come to that. Tosha was his heart, and he couldn't have it broken again. He needed Tosha whole because she completed him. Just thinking about how selfless she was in honoring Pearl's memory left him speechless.

"Please, Lord, I ask in your name, let this all work together for our good. That's what your word says, and I believe it. You know our needs. You know what we can bear. I trust you, Lord. Thank You for Your mercy and grace. In Jesus name, amen." Dewayne and Carl, the security guard and driver, said *amen* behind their pastor's prayer. Titus felt better about what he was to face as the car turned on his mother's street. He glanced toward his mother's home, and his heart seemed to go still as he saw lights from an ambulance parked in her driveway. Behind the ambulance was the car he recalled Brian Jackson driving. Without giving it a moment's thought, Titus opened the car door, although it was still moving, and jumped out, running toward his mother's house. The screams of Carl and Dewayne fell on deaf ears as he ran toward the front door. Before he could make it up the steps, the door flew open and out rushed medical personnel pushing his mother on a gurney. His world seemed to stop on its axis. His mother looked ashen as they rolled her past him. What had happened? He was pulled out of his frozen state when a hand touched his shoulder. Titus turned to see who touched him; it was Brian.

"Pastor, I know you have questions. I'll explain it all, but they say Eunice may have suffered a stroke and heart attack. We need to get to the hospital." Titus nodded in agreement and ran toward the ambulance. He stopped at his mother's side and looked to the paramedics who were loading her gurney.

"I'm her son. May I ride with her?"

"Yes, get in, hurry."

Titus jumped into the van and yelled over his shoulder to his men, "Follow us to the hospital and call my wife."

Act·Seven

Episode Fifty

Tosha and Tina could hardly wait for the automatic doors to the emergency room to open. Tosha felt like pounding on the doors, but finally, they opened. She asked Tina to ride with her to the hospital when she received the call from Deacon Dewayne. He informed her that Mother Eunice had some type of attack and that Titus wanted her to meet him at the hospital. Dewayne insisted that security drive them. She didn't understand the need as the threat was clearly down for the count. Nevertheless, she relented so that there would be no delay in her being with Titus in his time of need. There was also the suspense of how Summer's alleged father was involved. She and Tina ran through the doors and were immediately met by Titus and Dewayne, who both took their wives by their hands and ushered them into a waiting area.

"Honey, how is your mom?" Tosha asked with concern.

"They have her in surgery. She has a heart blockage. After the tests had revealed her heart wasn't getting the blood it needs to function, they decided she needed emergency surgery." Tosha, although an oncologist, understood the difference between mild, medium, and severe. She asked the question to determine what Eunice was facing.

"What range did the doctor say the blockage appeared to be?"

"He said eighty-five percent." Tosha's own heart slammed against her chest, and she reached to hug her husband. It didn't matter what trouble Eunice had caused them, it didn't prosper, and the very ill woman was still her husband's mother. She comforted her husband as best she could, trying to assure him that everything would be all right. Dewayne and Tina gave hugs and their own words of comfort. The group was disrupted when they heard a voice call out to them.

"Excuse me, Pastor Titus, can I have a moment with you?" Brian asked with a tremble in his voice. Titus looked at the man that couldn't have been older than he was.

"You can have a moment of my time in my family's presence. How do you know my mother, and what does this have to do with your paternity of Summer?" Titus was not about playing any games or delaying the truth. Something was off, and he wanted answers immediately. Brian and everyone in the room could feel the alpha persona radiate from Titus.

"There is not a chance of me being Summer's father. Eunice came up with that story to save you from making a mistake of continuing your marriage to Dr. Smith. She convinced me you were grieving and wanted a family so badly you just jumped at the first thing available."

Tosha wanted to slap Brian for just *repeating* something so vile about her. She was a highly sought after doctor for goodness sake. *What was wrong with these people*. However, she would not make the same mistake twice. She kept her cool and listened.

"So, that was enough for you to partner with my mother, a woman you don't know, to save me . . . what, as your pastor?" Titus was trying to make sense of this story.

"No, I was not operating as a member of KBM. I was acting as a lover trying to make my woman happy." Brian paused in his story, allowing Titus to digest what he had dished out. Titus didn't flinch the way everyone else in the room did.

"How long have you been my mother's lover?"

"Eleven years, since I was twenty."

"What does she provide for you?"

Brian looked at the floor ashamed of how he would be viewed when he answered. "Everything."

"Brian, I don't need to hear anymore. My mother has preyed on you. Just know if she makes it out of here, she won't have the means to provide for your lifestyle. So, you choose now if you are in or out with her. If you are in, she is going to need you to help her with her recovery. If you two were just using each other, walk away now—I won't sue you for the distress you caused my family with the fake claim of paternity."

It hurt Titus to his core to see Brian walk out of the hospital without a second thought.

Tosha went over to her husband and wrapped her arms around his waist to comfort him. He closed his eyes and returned her embrace, kissing her on top of her head. They stood there for long moments, only realizing they were not alone when the doctor entered the room.

"Doctor, what's the status of my mother?" Titus asked. The doctor looked up at Titus, who was taller than him, and recognized him as the pastor of Kingdom Building Ministry. The doctor had also worked on a team with Tosha in the past.

"Hello, Dr. Hightower. I didn't realize this was your family." He said scanning the room.

"Yes, Dr. Lee, this is my family. I'm now Dr. Hightower Smith. This is my husband, Pastor Titus Smith. Your patient, Eunice, is my mother-in-law."

"Very good, congratulations on your nuptials. I am happy to report that the patient, Eunice Smith, is now stable. We had to perform a double bypass on her heart, and she has seven stents. She suffered a mild stroke, but per her scans, we don't see any major damage. Once she wakes up, we will be able to do more tests and give you a more complete update. As for now, it will be slow, but she should make a full recovery." Titus released Tosha and went over to shake Dr. Lee's hand.

"Thank you, Dr. Lee. Can we see her now?"

"Yes, but only two at a time, and remember she may not be alert." Titus nodded his head in agreement and looked to Tosha. "Babe, are you coming with me?" Tosha didn't respond. She just walked up to her husband and took his hand, and they made their way out of the waiting room and into the corridor to see Mother Eunice.

***

The atmosphere of the room took Titus back to Pearl's final days, and his heart slammed against his chest. There lay his mother with an oxygen mask on her face and tubes running out of her arms and chest. The emotions that he felt took him by surprise. He was a pastor. He'd visited thousands of patients on their death beds. Although he had held his late wife's hand as she transitioned to glory, he was not prepared to see his mother fighting for her life. Titus' knees buckled as he made his way to her bed. Tosha was there by his side rubbing his back as he walked over to his mother. When he sat down at her bedside and cried, she was there comforting him and praying for him.

Titus felt Tosha's gentle hands rubbing his back. He was thankful for it. He felt her strength, and he was so happy to have this compassionate woman as his wife. His mother had been nothing but evil to her and their child, but Tosha was a saint. She turned the other cheek to all the fray his mother had caused them, and she was there loving him, loving them.

Titus took his mother's hand that had an I.V. attached to it and kissed it. He then got up and kissed her forehead. Then he prayed for healing.

"Father, we come crying out to you, Lord, in our time of trouble. We ask that you save us during this time of our distress. We decree the power of your word that by Your Stripes, Mother Eunice Smith is healed. We seek you to send out the angels to encamp around her, to heal her, and rescue her from this grave of spiritual death and blot out her transgressions. Touch her heart so that she may return to You and your righteousness. We give you thanks, oh Lord, for your unfailing love, and your wonderful works toward us. I lay hands on my mother as your word declares the Elders to do; I anoint her with oil and believe she shall recover. In the name of the Father, the Son, and the Holy Spirit. In Jesus name, we pray, amen."

Tosha took the holy oil she had given Titus as he laid hands on his mother and put it back in her purse. She had prayed fervently with her husband and had forgiven Mother Eunice, just like Titus and the Lord had forgiven Tosha for slapping Eunice several months ago. She sat in the room silently with her husband until it was time for her to go pick up Summer. That was the one silver lining in this debacle. No one would be taking their daughter away from them. Titus walked her out to her car, as Tina and Deacon Dewayne had left for the evening. He opened the car door for her, fastened her seatbelt across her waist, and gave her a lingering kiss. When he pulled back, he leaned in forehead to forehead with her.

"Thank you, love, for being here. You gave me the strength to see my mother that way and pray for her. I don't think I could make it without you."

Tosha cupped his face in her hands and spoke softly to him. "Pastor Titus, you are an anointed man of God. You would be alright without me, but it is my honor and pleasure to be by your side. I am always here for you, love, no matter what."

Titus took her lips again, and it felt like her kiss was restoring his faith and strength. He didn't think he would ever feel this complete again. In fact, it was better than it was before. He pulled away from his wife and closed the door. She pushed the button to roll down her window, and he leaned in.

"Sweetheart, go get our child before we do something that no pastor and first lady should be doing in a parking lot."

Tosha felt her cheeks flush as her man gave her a smile that melted her core. She blew a kiss to him, rolled up the window, and backed out of her parking space. Titus stood there like a man in love and watched his heart drive away. He didn't go back into the hospital until the rear lights of her car were out of sight.

When Titus made it back into his mother's room, he was shocked to see Brian Jackson sitting by her bedside.

"I thought you had made the decision to go away."

Brian was startled by the baritone voice that came from Titus. He got to his feet.

"I just needed time to clear my head. I love Eunice, and even if she can't give me another dollar, I will not abandon her. I'll stay by her side."

"Is that so, how do you plan on supporting yourself and my mother who may not fully recover if she makes it at all?" Titus furrowed his brows and closed some of the distance between him and the young man who could have been his little brother. "I am assuming your time served in the armed forces was fabricated?"

"No, it wasn't. I did four years in the reserves. I wasn't stationed out of the country as I claimed, but I do have my degree and can work. Eunice didn't want me to work, so I didn't. But I love her, Pastor Titus, and I will do what it takes."

Titus wasn't sure if he believed him, but the young man was willing to lie and scheme for his lover. Titus shook off his thoughts and extended his hand to Brian for a handshake. He didn't want any negativity in the room where he believed God was working, and Titus could feel the spirit of healing in the room. The first requirement for healing to take place was forgiveness.

Episode Fifty-One

It would be days later before Mother Eunice gained consciousness. When she could speak to Titus and Brian, she asked for forgiveness and said the repentance prayer.

She also started to sing, and when she did, she sang with a raspy low voice like Mahaila Jackson and sang "My God is Real." Titus sang with his mother, while Brian sat still with tears in his eyes. He could not explain the feeling he had. It was one of emptiness, yet Brian didn't feel alone. He closed his eyes and embraced the lyrics of the beautiful duet. Titus held his mother's hand as they sang.

Yes, God is real
Oh, He's real in my soul
Yes, God is real
For He has washed
And made me whole
Ooh, his love for me
Is just like pure gold, oh Lord
My God is real
For I can feel
Him in my soul

Titus paused as his mother sang with a strong voice like she had possessed in her youth.

His love for me-me
Is like pure gold.
My God is real
For I can, For I can
Feel him in my souuul.

Mother Eunice gasped holding her chest as the monitors beeped, and the medical staff rushed in. Twenty minutes later, Titus and Brian witnessed the doctor pronounce the time of death at eighteen hundred hours.

Titus was there to catch Brian as he lost control of all his emotions. He held the young man and assured him that he would one day love again.

***

Titus entered his home to a pleasant aroma of Italian herbs. Tosha was preparing her delicious spaghetti and meatballs. It had become his and Summer's favorite meal. He entered the kitchen where he saw his wife and daughter in matching aprons working together to put breadsticks in the oven. Summer was holding the oven door open as Tosha was putting the bread pan in. It was the best way to come home after losing his mother. Summer was the first to notice him, and she left her post before closing the oven door. She ran to her daddy and jumped in his arms. Tosha walked toward the pair, taking in her man's demeanor and assessing his mental and emotional state.

"Hi, Daddy, I'm sorry you lost your mommy. But, mommy said she is up there with my real mom, and they both are looking out for our family." Titus kissed his daughter on the forehead.

"Thank you, sweet-pea, and Mommy is right. I know I can get through this because you have showed me how to be brave after losing your real mom."

Titus was sincere in his words and squeezed her tightly while she hugged his neck. He placed Summer on her feet, and Tosha was the next body he had to hold in his arms for comfort. This woman's scent gave him strength to go on. Tosha embraced Titus then stood on her tiptoes to kiss him on the lips. She pulled away and searched his eyes. Titus felt like she could see his every thought and into his heart and soul.

"Are you okay, honey? Is there something you need me to do? Are you hungry?"

"I didn't think I could eat until I came in and smelled my favorite meal and saw my best girls. Dinner with you two is exactly what I need."

"Then go wash up, and when you return, dinner will be served."

"Yeah, Daddy, we have your favorite pecan pie for dessert." Titus smiled and winked at them both. He turned to go freshen up, feeling like everything was going to be all right.

The Smiths had a nice dinner, and they all cleaned the kitchen together after dessert. Titus and Tosha gave in to a game of Chutes and Ladders and read some chapters of *Charlotte's Web* before Summer was finally sleeping.

For the remainder of the evening, Tosha ministered to her husband as only a wife can. She drew him a bath and was there to dry him off when he stepped out of their large whirlpool tub. She had his Ralph Lauren pajama bottoms laid out to put on as she prepared to give him a massage with oil. However, Titus took the oil out of her hand,

captured her mouth, and took her. The massage would have
been nice, but he needed all of her to be the soothing balm
for his grief. Tosha obliged and gave him all of herself until
he was fast asleep in their bed of love.

After that night, Titus and Tosha, with the help of
their assistants Deacon Dewayne and Sister Tina, planned
the home-going ceremony for Mother Eunice.

One afternoon, while he was alone, Titus sat,
thinking about his departed mother and what he had
uncovered since her death. Titus was heartbroken at what
the financial audit revealed—his mom had stolen close to
one-million dollars to support her and her young lover's
lifestyle. He, being a man of great discernment, felt like he
should have known she was skimming off the top of the
church. Just as quickly as that thought came, another one
superseded it. His mother had been doing it for years, even
before his father died, and it was never brought to his
attention after he took over as lead pastor. From the
moment he had taken over, his mind had been on the
ministry and wooing Pearl. After they were married and
found out they couldn't have children, healing Pearl had
been at the forefront. And then . . . then Pearl had been ill
and passed away.

Moreover, as the pastor, he left the audits up to the accountants and unless someone came up to him and said, "Pastor, there is something funny about the finances." How would he have known?

"I didn't know, and that's an oversight I will have to live with," Titus said to himself and decided to let the matter go. They would not make the results of the audit public. His mother was gone. He would let her rest in peace. Titus was there when his mother repented, and he did not want her memory soiled by her late-life transgressions.

Brian promised that he did not know she was stealing the money as Eunice had always provided for him since their affair began. Titus had no reason not to believe Brian. The affair had started so early and gone on so long that his mother had truly violated the young man. Brian would undoubtedly need counseling after the relationship he had with Titus' mother and her death. He recommended to Brian that he attend counseling at KBM's partner ministry, Liberty Fellowship Church. After several weeks, he learned Barbara Stoneheart and Brian had begun seeing each other. Tosha told him not to interfere because it was apparent that Brian preferred older women, and at least this time, she wasn't an old woman. Titus let it go. So many other things were taking place in their lives. The best being that the paperwork had come through from the court and Summer Harvey was officially Summer Harvey Smith.

Episode Fifty-Two

"Surprise!" Summer turned around and ran to her father's leg wrapping her arms around them as tightly as she could. Titus reached down and pried her arms loose and picked her up. She was frightened by all the people who jumped out from all directions of their home. They had just returned home from seeing the latest Pixar movie.

"Sweet Pea, don't be afraid." Titus turned her head so she could face her audience. "See, these are our family and friends here to celebrate with you for becoming Summer Harvey Smith." Summer's eyes widened, and a smile appeared on her beautiful face. Gone was the scared little girl, in her place was a princess. She crossed her arms over her heart, batted her eyes and said, "This is all for meee?"

"Yes, honey, for you." Tosha spoke up with mirth in her voice. "Now, let Dad put you down and greet your guests." Titus stood Summer on her feet and watched his little princess come to life.

"Excuse my behavior, everyone. I was caught off guard by your presence. I'm delighted that you have come to celebrate me." Summer said with a British accent, and the guests laughed out loud. The little girl was destined to be a drama queen. They all rushed in to hug and kiss on her. After getting over the initial shock, Summer soaked up all the attention from everyone. Her grandma and grandpa Hightower were there with gifts like it was her birthday.

"Grandma and Grandpa, I didn't know I would get gifts too," Summer said as she tore into the gift boxes.

"You most certainly do. This is your second birthday. The first was when you were born to your mother, Olivia, and you were named Summer Harvey. Today, we are celebrating you being Summer Harvey Smith, and that includes gifts." Mrs. Hightower smiled down at Summer not sure she had heard a word that was spoken to her as she was jumping up and down with her new tablet.

"Thank you, Grandma and Papa. Now, I can video chat with you every night." Summer hugged each of her grandparents not letting go of her gift.

The evening only became brighter for Summer as she embraced her family and received more gifts than she had in all the Christmases of her life. She shouted exclamations as she was opening presents from the Owens,

who came with more extended family—the District
Attorney, Kevin Michelson, with his wife Paige and their
infant daughter, Moriah, and their niece, Nikki. Paige was
Seth's niece who had formed a bond with Janine and
Tosha. The Douglas' were there, as usual, to support them
with members of the congregation that had children in
Summer's Sunday School class. Summer's next destination
was in the back yard with her classmates, Hope, Charity,
and Nikki. They jumped in the bouncing house, rode the
merry-go-round, and flying airplane rides, Titus had
insisted on renting.

Summer excused herself from her friends and went
to her bedroom. Her parents saw and followed her,
stopping at her closed door after she entered. Tosha cracked
the door slightly open, so that they could hear. They
watched Summer go to her nightstand and pick up the
picture of Olivia.

"Hi, Mommy, I know you can hear me in heaven. I
just want to say thank you for picking me the best Mommy
and Daddy. I miss you every day, but I am with our family,
and they are taking care of me. I love Mommy and Daddy
so much, and I know they love me. So, does Grandpa and
Grandma Hightower, not just because they gave me a
tablet, but because they give me love. I will never forget

you, Momma, and I didn't want you to miss out on the party, so I came to tell you about it. Now, I must go back outside and make sure my little cousins Hope and Charity are okay. Oh! I made a new friend, Nikki Jones. She is older than me by a little bit, but she said I don't act my age. Anyway, Mommy, I'll talk to you tonight."

Tosha and Titus scurried away from the door, dashing into the powder room across the hall. They both had tear-stained faces. Summer was proving to be wise beyond her years.

"Our little girl is such a blessing." Tosha cried. Titus wrapped his loving arms around her nodding his shaven head in agreement. "I couldn't love her more if I had her myself."

"I agree. When I look at her, I see my little girl. You and Summer are such a gift to me, Babe. I couldn't ask for anything more." He kissed the top of his wife's head as she cried. This was not the first time they had peeked in when Summer spoke to Olivia, but this was the most emotional. Tosha couldn't speak. If she did, she would break down sobbing.

"You okay, babe?" He asked in concern.

"Yes, I'm fine. It's just you said you couldn't ask for anything more." Titus frowned. *What was wrong with that statement?* He wondered but didn't say anything. Maybe it was her time of the month. "Sweetheart, you have come into my life and given me more than I could have hoped or imagined. I'm happy with all that we have been blessed with." Tosha pulled back and considered his eyes.

"Could you be happy with a baby?" In shock, Titus dropped his arms and took his wife's hands into his, looking her over from her head to her feet.

"Tosha, are you pregnant?"

She nodded her head in the affirmative. "Yes, I am, about four to six weeks. We may have conceived on our wedding night."

"Aw, baby, you are giving me a baby!" Titus picked his wife up in a hug. "The Lord is truly blessing us. This is wonderful news. Thank you, Tosha, for being the most amazing woman. I love you, Summer and our little one growing so much."

"We love you too." Titus wiped the tears from Tosha's face with his thumbs. He picked up a washcloth and wet it so that he could wash all the remnants away.

"Let's get you freshened up. Our guests are probably searching for us." Tosha closed her eyes as he washed her face like she was Summer's age, but she didn't mind. This man of hers was Heaven sent.

***

Later that night, after Summer was nestled in bed, Tosha and Titus were lying in a spooning position. Titus' hand was splayed across Tosha's stomach as he caressed the area that housed his growing baby while they enjoyed some pillow talk.

"Summer was truly surprised today." Tosha spoke in a sleepy voice.

"Yes, she had a ball tonight. When I tucked her in, she told me she was exhausted, so we could skip the book reading."

"Yep, she was tired then if she didn't want Daddy to read to her. Oh, Titus, she is such a sweet girl and precious to me."

Titus kissed the side of his wife's face and moved down to her neck. In between the kisses, he whispered in her ear. "You are precious to me, and I thank God you are mine, that Summer is mine." Gently massaging her stomach, he went under the covers to plant a kiss on her now flat tummy. "Our child that is growing inside of you is precious to me, and I love all three of you with all that I am," Titus declared as he positioned Tosha back against his flesh, wrapping his arms around her as they spooned.

"Babe, you say the sweetest things. The three of us are blessed to have you."

There was a long pause as Titus held his love tighter and kissed the top of her head. "We should get some sleep. Tonight was just one event out of two we had to prepare for." Tosha raised her head and looked over her shoulder at Titus.

"You're right. I have so many deliverables to check off before the dedication of the health center next weekend. I believe Tina and I have most of it under control," Tosha said while yawning. "All the Oncology medical professionals have confirmed attendance, so we have to figure out how many will be able to speak."

"You haven't finalized the program yet?" Titus asked with concern. "Do you need help from Sister Yvette? She is free because I have not replaced the position my mother held."

"No, we are almost done. I will send you the rough draft on Monday." Tosha stretched and murmured. "I'm tired, honey. Today was beautifully exhausting, and tomorrow, we have church all day." Before Titus could respond and tell her to attend the late service only if she wanted, he heard Tosha's even breathing and felt her body relax into his. His lady was asleep. He would tell her in the morning to sleep in. He took the nightly position he had since they were married. He buried his face into the back of her neck, and before a minute passed, he was asleep too.

Episode Fifty-Three

Tosha sat at her desk listening to JJ Hairston's "You Deserve It." As she went over the itinerary for the dedication of the facility, she allowed the lyrics of the song to minister to her. The words had an impact on her until she had to put the report she was reading down. Her eyes were full of tears as she swayed in her chair to the melody and sang with words of praise that were true in her heart.

All the glory belonged to God. He deserved it. Tosha was not looking for love when she applied for the position at Pearl's Health Facility. She wasn't looking to become a mother when she served Olivia Harvey in her last days. But God rewarded her with the desires of her heart. He answered prayers she hadn't dared spoken out loud. Her Hallelujah belonged to Him for he had blessed her beyond all that she could imagine. He deserved her praise. Tosha lifted her hands in worship in her office. *All* the glory belonged to God.

"Excuse me, Dr. Smith . . ." Tosha opened her eyes then grabbed a Kleenex from her desk. She sat up straight in her seat.

"Come in, Tina. I just got caught up and became emotional." Tosha decided to leave it there. She and Titus discussed waiting until she was farther along in her pregnancy to make the reveal. Tina gave her a look of concern. It wasn't like Tosha to sit in her office and cry, but she decided to let it go.

"Well, I wanted you to know I received the RSVP from Dr. Avery Gentry." Tina waited for a response. She knew that name would weigh heavy on her girl.

Dr. Avery Gentry was Tosha's first love. They dated for several years, separating because of the directions of their careers. Dr. Avery was the Head of Surgery at the School of Medicine in Memphis and had been extended an invitation.

Tosha swallowed and then looked up and said, "You received it this early in the mail? It's not even noon yet. What did the letter say?" Tosha asked picking up her thermos of coffee. She closed her eyes as she drank. As soon as it hit her tongue, she was in heaven with the caramel taste.

"Mr. Dave hasn't delivered the mail yet."

"Oh, did he accept via email?"

"No, he delivered it personally."

"He what?" Tosha asked with wide eyes. "Avery is here?"

"Yes, ma'am, in the flesh, and he would like to see you. Although, I'm not sure that is wise because you look a little off. You sure everything is okay with you?" Tina walked closer to Tosha's desk examining her boss and friend. She would think that the news of Avery's visit had Tosha pale, but she was that way when Tina entered.

"Are you okay, Tosha? You look flushed? Was it the devotion, or is the good pastor keeping you up late at night?" Tina joked.

Tosha waved her off and stood, smoothing down her dress. She had on a simple, black fitted dress with ankle booties on. "I'm not going there with you, Tina, use your imagination," Tosha said with a wink. "I'll be happy to meet with Avery. I will go out to him. Can you buzz Titus and have him come to my office if he is free?"

Tina looked bewildered. "What?" Tosha stopped, as Tina asked, "You sure you want to introduce your new husband to your ex?"

Tosha continued her stride, speaking as she walked and Tina followed. "Don't be silly. I would like the esteemed doctor to meet the pastor of KBM and the Founder of Pearl's Health facility."

Tina had remained quiet although she thought, *and you want to show him how well you did despite him dumping you for someone who would stroke his ego and much more.* But Tina didn't say any of that, she went back to her desk and did as she was asked.

Dr. Avery Gentry was always impeccably dressed. He was six feet two with skin that looked as if it had been gently kissed by the sun. His dark brown eyes appeared mysterious when he held someone in his gaze. When he smiled, he had the straightest white teeth that appeared to have a sparkle to them. Tosha walked into the foyer where Avery was admiring the artwork. The sound of her heels made him turn and behold her.

Tosha straightened her back and walked toward her past. "Hello, Avery, thank you for coming by to accept our invitation," Tosha said with a smile as she extended her hand.

"Girl, I don't want a handshake," Avery said as he pulled Tosha into his body for an embrace. She tried to step out of the hold he had on her, but she wasn't strong enough to break away. Avery held her tightly and inhaled her personal fragrance. "Tosha, you feel and smell the same. I've missed you."

Before she could respond or push him off of her, she heard a baritone voice that sent shivers down her spine.

"Who do we have here with their arms around my beloved?" Titus asked as he strolled up to the two engaged in a hug. He pulled Tosha's arm out of Avery's hold and squinted his eyes toward the man who would dare hold his wife that closely. Avery lifted his hands in surrender.

"I'm sorry. I haven't seen, Tosh, in a while. I was just excited to see her, no disrespect meant." Avery extended his hand. "I'm Dr. Avery Gentry. I received the invitation to the dedication and came to accept personally."

Titus took Avery's hand into a death grip and gave a warning smile. "I am Titus Smith, lead pastor here and the husband of the woman you just had your arms around."

"Sweetheart, Dr. Avery and I went to med school together."

"Now, Tosh, we did more than go to med school." Tosha thought she would melt where she stood.

"Okay, we dated for a while but nothing serious. We are happy you can attend the dedication."

"Yes, we are. If you would like a private tour of the facility, I will have a staff member escort you. Otherwise, thanks for coming, and we will see you at the dedication service later this week," Titus decreed letting the good doctor know there was nothing else for him there.

Avery had no comeback, so he shook Titus' hand again. "I'll wait until the dedication for the tour. It was nice to meet you, Pastor, and, Tosh, I'll catch up with you later."

Titus wanted to beg to differ, but since Avery scampered away, he watched him leave. When Avery was out of sight, he looked down at Tosha.

"Are you okay, honey? Why did you send for me to meet him?"

"I just wanted you close. We didn't end on the best of terms, and I just wanted you near me while I spoke to him."

"It looked like he wanted to do more than speak. I don't like how he handled you. What went on with him?" Tosha stood on her tiptoes and kissed Titus on the lips. "It doesn't matter. Avery is gone, and I don't want to think about that time in my life."

"Honey, why did you allow him to be invited if you aren't comfortable with him. I can uninvite him." Titus looked at her with furrowed brows trying to figure out what was up with her and Dr. Gentry. They hadn't had in-depth conversations about her previous relationships because she said there weren't any that serious. Obtaining her medical degree had been her top priority. Finding out she was a virgin when they married validated that there was no one special in her past. Still, walking up on his woman being held tightly by another man made him think they needed to have a heart-to-heart about this guy. He started to say so, but Tosha collapsed so quickly he barely caught her.

"Tina!" he yelled as he picked his wife up and entered her office, lying her on the couch. Tina ran in behind them.

"What's wrong with her, Pastor?"

"I think she just got a little light-headed," Titus answered as he removed his wife's shoes and gently placed her legs and feet on the sofa. He got up. "I'm going to get her a cool towel for her head. Can you call one of the doctors to come check her vitals?"

"Yes, sir," Tina said while circling around Tosha's desk to her phone. She paged Dr. Jeffries, a primary physician, employed by KBM for the health facility. Tina could not figure out why Titus was so calm. But as Dr. Jeffries rushed in and spoke with Titus, she found out.

"I think she may need something to eat. She was standing and just fainted. She is about six weeks pregnant, and knowing her, she's only had that latte in that thermos on her desk," Titus said as Tina gasped and started clapping. Dr. Jeffries was beginning to take Tosha's vitals when she awoke.

"What happened?" She asked, alarmed that she was lying on her couch with Dr. Jeffries probing her.

"Have you eaten anything today, Dr. Smith?"

"No, not yet. Did I faint? I was going to get a bagel, but I had a guest to arrive then Titus . . . oh, I guess I did faint," she said sheepishly, ashamed of the fact that she was careless. She was a doctor for crying out loud. "I'll be fine, Dr. Jeffries. I'll have something to eat and hydrate, I promise."

Dr. Jeffries immediately stopped and gathered his bag. Dr. Smith had all but dismissed him. He stood to leave, and Tina stood as well. She watched as Dr. Jeffries left the room.

"Tosha, I'm not going to say anything about you not telling me I'm about to be a TT again. But do either of you need anything from me?" Tina asked looking from Tosha to Titus.

"No, Sister Tina, that will be all. I'm going to take my wife home and feed her lunch and put her to bed."

"No, Titus, I have a ton of work to do. I can't go home for the day."

"Too bad, you should have eaten. Now you are in my care, and it's home, lunch, and rest."

"Now, be a good wife and submit to your husband." Tina teased. Tosha rolled her eyes.

"Weren't you leaving?"

"Yes, I am. I'll call and check on you later." Tina said and exited the room racing to her desk to call Dewayne. He had better not have known and didn't tell her.

Later that evening, after Titus had taken care of Tosha, they broke the news that Summer was going to be a big sister. They celebrated over chicken-noodle soup and read several Curious George books. Summer was finally out for the night in her bedroom. Titus was stroking Tosha's hair, as her head lay on his chest, when he brought up Dr. Avery Gentry.

"So, tell me what happened between you and Avery Gentry." Tosha closed her eyes as she realized he had not forgotten about the scene he walked in on earlier. She didn't raise her head but asked quietly, "What do you want to know?"

"I want to know why you are afraid of him, and why it looked like you were accustomed to him manhandling you."

"That's just how he is. To become the head of surgery for a hospital, you have to be a person in control. That is Avery's strength and weakness. He would try to control me, and when I didn't allow it, he would sometimes try other methods rather than manipulating words." Titus continued to stroke her hair, wanting her to remain comfortable in revealing the truth he suspected.

"Did he hit you?"

Tosha was so ashamed to admit it. She was a woman who had kept her sexual virtue intact but failed to protect herself emotionally and physically.

"Sometimes, he would," she whispered.

"He hit you?" Titus asked again. He needed to hear her say that joke-of-a-man had abused her.

"Yes, Titus, he would hit me sometimes. But I told myself it was the pressure of medical school and his need to please his family. I know it was weak of me. He was willing to wait for sex until marriage, and I thought prayer would help him."

"Did it?"

"It did some, and the fact that I made sure I stayed busy with my study groups, labs, and volunteer work. When Avery caught on to how I was avoiding him, he gave me an ultimatum to leave school and marry him. He said I could finish up after him. That my focus needed to be on him and his needs. When I refused, it got physical, and I ended up at the bottom of a flight of stairs. The fall broke my arm, and I promised not to press charges against him if he would let me go."

"So, that's why you called for me. And from the looks of it, he was ready to drag you out of the building this morning. Tosha, listen to me and listen good. That *man* is not welcome on any property that I own or govern. He will not be attending the dedication service. I'll let him know personally." Tosha bolted up with a concerned look.

"Titus, please leave it alone. No one knows but you, me, and him. I never told a soul. I lied to Tina about my broken arm. Just let him come, and I won't go anywhere near him."

"Sweetheart, you are my wife, the mother of my child, and pregnant with another one. There is no way that man is coming within a foot of you. I'm a man of peace, but I will protect what's mine until death. Now lie back down, I'm getting cold without you." Tosha laid her head back down on his chest and closed her eyes as he began to rub her hair again. She decided to let it go and went to sleep feeling loved and protected.

Episode Fifty-Four

As the days passed, Titus pondered the events of Tosha's past. He could calm himself because Tosha was safe, and Avery was not a factor in their day-to-day life. He had nixed the idea of banning him from attending the dedication. His wife knew how to handle herself. She had showed that by immediately sending for him after knowing she would encounter this doctor who paraded around like a pillar of the community. Titus felt any man that would harm a woman was a fraud, and the truth was not in him. There were other pressing matters at hand besides opening the clinic and the normal stressors that come with being a pastor, a new husband, and father. One of them was, for the last week, his precious wife was on her knees every morning emptying the contents of her stomach for over an hour.

These days, Titus would stand in the doorway of their bathroom as Tosha finished her new morning routine. He would watch as she flushed and stumbled her way over to the sink to wash out her mouth and wash her things. The poor thing had to wait until later in the morning to brush her teeth because that action would send her back to her knees. The first morning Tosha experienced morning sickness, Titus was on the floor with her, rubbing her back.

She pushed him away stating that irritated her more. Now, he waited at the door with a bottle of ginger ale and crackers. This had been their new normal, and he would continue to stand there until this morning sickness passed. He prayed it was soon. He often had flashbacks of Pearl's retching after chemotherapy and had to remind himself this was not the same. After this suffering, they would experience new life, not death. That was why he stood patiently waiting for her to accept her breakfast.

Tosha turned off the faucet and picked up the towel to dry her hands. She turned and smiled at her loving husband. She had no idea why his touch in the early morning irritated her. She was happy it only lasted a little while and that Titus understood. She walked toward the door and smiled as he moved to give her room to walk through. She climbed back up into their high mahogany sleigh bed and got underneath the covers. When she seemed settled, Titus sat down beside her and opened the bottle of chilled ginger ale and crackers. Tosha drank the soda then nibbled on the crackers. They sat in silence for long minutes to see if it digested.

"Thank you, sweetheart. I think we have survived another round of morning sickness."

Titus leaned in a kissed her forehead.

"Praise the Lord, now lie down and get a nap. I will get Summer off to school. It worked out great that they are having an arts and crafts day on a Saturday, and I'll swing back to get you so that we can go in to the office together." Tosha scooted down farther into the bed thinking she would sleep for an hour, and then get up and prepare for the dedication this afternoon.

Titus gathered the empty bottle and wrapper from the crackers and left his wife to rest. They had a busy day, and he hoped that Tosha was up for it, but first, he had to make sure the little princess was taken care of. He closed the door to their master suite and headed toward Summer's room.

"Time to wake up, princess." Titus smiled down as Summer stretched, balling her fists up and then rubbing her eyes with them. Finally, she opened her eyes and saw her dad.

"Good morning, Daddy, is it time for me to get ready for school already?" Summer asked as she sat up then immediately fell back on her pillow and picked up her favorite doll. Titus took the doll out of her hand and placed it on the pillow next to her. Then he picked Summer up as if she was a two-year-old versus five.

"Yes, princess, and now, you have to go and wash your face, brush your teeth, and put on your lotion." Titus deposited her on her feet in her personal restroom decorated with a Doc McStuffins shower curtain and Doc McStuffins rugs and towels. "When you are done, go back to your room, put on your school uniform, and come down for breakfast."

"Are you making my oatmeal with fruit?" Summer asked as if her completing his demands were contingent upon her breakfast menu.

"Yes, princess, if that is what you would like. Oatmeal with fruit toppings, toast, and orange juice is what you shall have." Summer smiled and picked up the towel Tosha had laid out for her. Every night, after Tosha bathed Summer and put her to bed, she prepared Summer's restroom for her to freshen up the next morning easily. Summer's school uniform was on a chair in her bedroom with her tights and shoes underneath the chair. Summer's hair was natural unruly curls, so, at night, Tosha combed it up in a ponytail and put a silk bonnet on her hair. After Summer dressed in the morning, she took the bonnet off and placed a headband of her choice on her head. Then she would head to breakfast, and Titus would take her to school. This morning didn't deviate from that routine. After breakfast, Titus carried Summer into their bedroom and leaned her over to kiss her mommy on the forehead. Tosha turned over and embraced her.

"Have a great day at school, sweetie," Tosha said weakly.

"I will, Mommy. Did my baby sister or brother make you sick again?" Summer asked with a slight frown on her face, waiting for her mom to respond.

"Yes, a little bit, but I'm feeling better now. I just need a nap then I will be good." That seemed to satisfy Summer.

"Ok, get your rest before Daddy takes you to work."

"I will."

Titus leaned down and kissed Tosha on the forehead, and they were off to begin their day.

Episode Fifty-Five

Looking at Tosha give her opening speech on stage at the dedication service of Pearl's Health Facility (PHF), no one could possibly know the battle with morning sickness she had experienced hours earlier. Titus looked on with pride as she delivered a beautiful presentation on the priorities of PHF. When she completed her speech, she ended the presentation with a drop-down canopy poster of

the late Mrs. Pearl Smith in an evening gown that Tosha
had found in the attic. There were gasps and covered
mouths. Titus' knees buckled at the beautiful portrait that
waved like a flag. He went up to his wife and gave her a
passionate kiss like the one on their wedding day. When the
crowd noticed the kiss, the volume of the applause went up
a hundredfold. The participants were clapping and
stomping; it was a beautiful sight to behold.

In the corner of the foyer stood Dr. Avery Gentry
envy and greed filled his eyes. That was his woman up
there, and he had to have her again. She was an oncologist
who had become—*what a preacher's wife and charity
worker now?* No way, his girl deserved more than that.
With devious thoughts running through his mind, he put his
hands together and clapped for the couple and the opening
of the center. He laughed a little thinking how small
minded it was of Tosha to walk in the shadow of this man's
late wife. He would have to bring her to her senses.

Tosha and Titus spent the afternoon mingling,
shaking hands, and thanking their guests for supporting
their cause and for the financial gifts. The benevolence that
was given was outstanding. Donations ranged from five
thousand dollars to fifty thousand. They were blown away,

and Tosha couldn't wait until they started accepting patients next week.

Titus was in a huddle speaking to Pastor Derrick Caine, Minister Seth Owens, and a gentleman who was introduced to him as Benjamin Adams. In the middle of his sentence, he felt a tap on his shoulder. When he looked around, his smile disappeared from his face. It was Dr. Avery Gentry; the last man he wanted to see. Being the man of integrity that he was, Titus shook Avery's hand and introduced him to the others in the group. Avery was polite and greeted the other men in the group before turning to Titus. "May I have a word with you in private, Pastor?" Titus nodded his head in agreement and excused himself from the group.

"Please follow me, Dr. Gentry. We can have a word in my office." Avery followed Titus, preparing his approach on how to get back into the one that slipped away's life. He was under a lot of stress back in medical school and didn't treat Tosh like the lady she was. But now, he had his anger in check, and he knew he could win her heart back. Surely, she didn't love this preacher more than him. Avery was even willing to overlook her being tainted by this man's touch.

"Would you like to have a seat?" Titus asked Avery, breaking him out of his reverie.

"No thanks, I'll be brief. I just wanted to say how impressed I am with your health facility." Avery opened his suit coat and pulled out an envelope. He passed it over to Titus. Titus received the envelope and opened it. The twenty-five-thousand-dollar cashier's check inside caused him to look at Avery with a raised eyebrow.

"This is quite a contribution."

"I feel it fits the vision you have here, and, Pastor Smith, I would love to assist if you have room on your board or volunteer staff." Titus furrowed his brow as he stared at the man in front of him. *Was this guy nuts?* Titus closed some of the space between them and spoke smoothly.

"Dr. Gentry this is a generous gift; nonetheless, I must decline if you think this is an open door to my wife."

Avery let out a low chuckle. "Of course, I would love spending time with Tosh, but this is a worthy cause, and I would like to help financially and with my time. Catching up with Tosha is just icing on the cake."

Titus did not like this man's spirit at all, and he was never one to play head games or mix words.

"Listen, Dr. Avery. I know all about your history with my wife, or Tosh as you call her. I know what you did to her, and how a fall down the stairs of her apartment ended your relationship." Titus pushed the envelope into Avery's chest and stood toe to toe, chest to chest, and eye to eye with his opponent.

"You can take this check and donate it somewhere else. You, and it, are not welcome on these grounds."

Avery was caught off guard by Titus' bluntness but quickly recovered.

"So, this is how a man of the cloth responds to charity? You assume I'm running a game trying to win back your wife?"

"Dr. Avery, make no mistake. I'm a God-fearing man, and I love my wife like Christ loves the church. Christ died for his bride the church, and I'm willing to do the same. I'll fight to the death any adversary that tries to harm her. Feel me?"

Avery felt every word and wanted to knock the pastor out for speaking to him in such a tone. But he was a medical professional, and he wasn't about to brawl in a church.

"Okay, I will take my gift back since it seems you think I have ill intentions. It's all good. My schedule is too full to be adding another volunteer board to my list. So, Pastor, it was a pleasure speaking to you, until the next time." Avery turned to leave only stopping when Titus called out to him.

"Dr. Gentry, there won't be a next time. Tosha is my wife and carrying my seed. You have no business here unless you are seeking salvation for your soul. Have a nice life."

Avery walked out feeling defeated until he saw Tosha and rage filled his veins. She was talking and laughing with a group of women, but her gaze met his, and she looked away quickly. Avery was sure Tosha had read his eyes and knew it wasn't over. The nerve of her not only marrying, and lying with another man, but conceiving a child! It wasn't over. Avery exited the building knowing he would return.

Tosha was delighted to see Avery leave, but she wondered what that private conversation was about. She would have to speak to Titus about it later. She had a building full of guests to cater to and had to find something to eat before she caused morning sickness to come in the afternoon.

"Lady Tosha, you okay?" Sister Yvette asked her first lady as she seemed flush.

"Yeah, Tosha are you okay?" Tina asked.

"Yes, I'm fine. I'm just going to go in the fellowship hall and have a bite to eat." Tina grabbed Tosha by the elbow, and Yvette took the other arm. Tosha wanted to protest but knew there was no use.

Upon entering the fellowship hall, she was pleasantly surprised to see Titus seated and motioning for her to join him. He was seated at a table with her parents, Pastor Derrick Caine, Barbara, Brian, Seth, Janine, Dewayne, and a couple she would later be introduced to, Benjamin and Camille Adams. Tosha smiled from ear to ear as Titus already had a plate of items she could tolerate. She took her seat next to her husband. He leaned in and said, "I love you so much. I praise God I found true love again."

Social Media Edition

As I stated earlier, I wrote the majority of Love Again as a mini-series in my Facebook group. When I would release a new post, I would sit in great anticipation of what the members would say. They are a group of readers that help bring the story to life. I would like to invite you to join our reader's group, click here: https://www.facebook.com/groups/gdwoodsbooks.

The next mini-series I will be writing for the readers group is *Recovered Through Love*. You can have a sneak peek from our hero below.

Recovered Through Love

A word from our hero:

Hello, my name is Pastor Derrick Caine, and I have a testimony. It is one about my life as a young man of the cloth and a husband, and how it all ended abruptly.

Some may call it a bit of a tragedy. I call it being tried by fire. Yes, that is what it feels like. Your insides are consumed by fire when your wife of twenty years says that she's leaving your marriage for someone else. That someone else being a woman is the match to your heart and soul that's already consumed by gasoline.

Emily was never a cruel woman. She was always kind and supportive to me and the ministry. If there were signs that she desired women, I missed every one of them.

There were no warning bells that rang in my ear. We were happy. I thought we were. So, it felt like my body exploded when she told me it was over, and that she was never happy in our marriage and preferred her best friend in all aspects. I didn't want to believe her. I didn't want the marriage to end. I had laid hands on the sick, and they had recovered. I prayed for people to find jobs and they did. I was a man of God, always trying to walk worthy in the vocation that I was called. Despite all those things, I found myself divorced at forty-two years old after twenty years of marriage.

What was I to do? I was preaching the gospel to thousands of souls a week in the sanctuary. I counseled young and old couples alike. How could I stand before God's people after my life had fallen to shambles? I asked myself, *do I leave the faith? Do I curse God for allowing this shame to come upon me? Do I hurt Emily for living a lie? What do I do?*

I stood still to seek the salvation of the Lord. I took months off to heal emotionally. I allowed my associate ministers to keep the congregation moving forward. I examined myself and took responsibility for not seeing what I should have. Emily didn't make demands for much in our marriage. She never asked me to slow down my travel or reduce my ministry hours so we could spend time together. I chose to believe that she was supportive and occupied herself with girlfriends for just friendly fellowship. I never questioned anything odd about her behavior because I was focused on my goals for the ministry. I was focused on making sure the members of Liberty Fellowship Church (LFC) were whole. I didn't look at my wife, the one I promised to forsake all others for and see that she was broken. I allowed her to remain torn instead of helping her mend. I neglected my own house. I neglected my priority, my wife, and it cost Emily and me. She has pulled out of all forms of Christianity and religion. I prayed, and continually do, that she and her companion make peace with Christ.

I will forever regret that for two decades I did not watch over my wife's soul. Still, I could not dwell in that regret forever. I decided nothing would separate me from the love of Christ, and I would continue to preach in season and out of season. I believed that the Lord would give me a chance to recover all that I had lost. Little did I know, I would recover it all through love.

The love of a wonderful woman has come into my life. She's suffered loss as well, and we've helped one another heal. I'm grateful for her and happy to share our story with you. I can't wait for you to find out who she is. Get ready to meet my second chance at love. My second chance to be who God has called me to be.

The telling of our story will go like this—I will share my point of view, and she will share hers. Sometimes, it will be about the same event, and others, it will be about our individual journeys. At the end, you will see how the Lord trades beauty for ashes and strength for fear. You will see him do a new work in me and my lady love. I'm so happy to have found her. She is a good thing.

So, get ready as GDWOODSBOOKS presents, *Recovered through Love.*

I am Pastor Derrick Caine

Bonus

Do you want to learn more about Seth and Janine Owens? As a bonus keep reading to discover more about forgiveness after infidelity in marriage.

GDWOODSBOOKS

PRESENTS

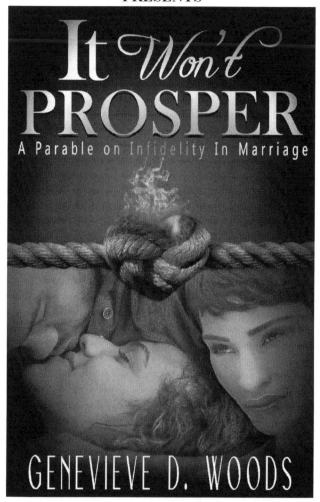

for subscribers to www.gdwoodsbooks.com

A GDWOODSBOOKS PUBLICATION

It Won't Prosper by Genevieve D. Woods
First Edition: October 2016

Episode One

Janine

I look at the pictures one by one, over and over for what feels like hours. *How could Seth do this to me, to what we have shared?* We've been married for five years and dated for two before vowing in front of God, family, and friends to love each other like no other could until the breath left our bodies. Looking at these pictures of him greeting another woman with a kiss that he promised only to be for me, enfolding her in the arms that are designed to comfort me, taking her by the hand and leading her into the hotel to consummate a relationship with the love that was to cover me—is heartbreaking. The pain is like none I've ever felt. A broken heart feels like a machete has torn into my chest and swiftly sliced my heart into a million unrecognizable pieces.

In that pile of pieces is my trust in him.
In that pile of pieces is my dream for forever.
In that pile of pieces is my joy.
In that pile of pieces is my peace.
In that pile of pieces is my future.
In that pile of pieces is my naivety.

What is not in that pile is my faith in God and the belief that all things work together for the good, for those who love the Lord and are called according to his purpose. For this cause, I bow my knees and pray to my Father in Heaven for guidance and direction. As I pray, the verse that says a husband is sanctified by his believing wife comes to my shattered heart, and I feel the power of the Spirit mending my broken heart. I am still devastated by his actions, but I have sinned and come short of the glory of God in many different areas of my life. I continue with my prayers to my Father in Heaven that His will be done in my life and my relationship. I pray until my tears turn into determination that this unholy woman will not have my husband. I pray until I am positive that this will not be the end of my union with the man I adore, Seth Owens. I will fight this spiritual wickedness that has come against the harmony of my life with the most powerful weapon created . . . the word of God. My eyes are open, and I see my husband is not perfect. He has fallen into temptation, but greater is He that is within me, and I will not allow this attack on my marriage to prosper. This woman had better have enjoyed these rendezvous; it will soon be over because she is about to be sidelined.

I finish my prayer by saying, "In Jesus name, I pray." I put the evidence of my husband's betrayal back in the envelope the private investigator gave me, and I rise to put it into the back of my closet. But not before I write on it, *no weapon formed against us shall prosper*. I leave my home office where I do freelance writing for several faith-based magazines and children's Christian books. I head toward the bathroom in the master bedroom that I share with my husband and proceed toward the shower. In the shower, I let the disappointment wash off of me, and I resolve I will keep my vows to my husband and love him, like no other can.

I'm in the kitchen cooking dinner when I hear our home alarm system alert that the front door is opening. I still can't get used to that monotone voice, but it is something he had to have. It's been a few hours since my shower, and I've completed another book to send to my editor entitled *Children's Church*. I am shocked to my core to see my tall, dark, and handsome husband enter the kitchen with a bouquet of beautiful flowers, but I wouldn't be honest if I did not admit I get butterflies in my stomach. I love my husband. When he comes over and pulls me by my waist into his toned body, images of the pictures enter my mind. However, I don't recoil from his embrace; I am the one who belongs in his arms, not her. He leans down to kiss me on the lips, and I return it completely, loving the taste that I have known for years that is a mixture of his unique scent and his favorite gum. I love my husband. We kiss like we're teenagers. Our kiss ends with the sound of the oven's timer. Our dinner is ready.

"Honey, this meal is delicious. Did you get any writing done today?"

"Yes, I finished *Children's Church*, completed some investigation projects, and even had some prayer time."

"Babe, you are everything. All that and you made my perfect meal, spaghetti and meatballs, fried chicken, green beans, yams, corn bread, and apple pie. I'm living the dream." He reaches over to me and puckers his lips for a kiss. I oblige. While kissing him, I know this is the reason it took a private investigator to make me accept the truth about my husband. Seth has always treated me like his queen. He never yells, even when we disagree. He has always been supportive of my dreams. When I told him I wanted to leave the six-figure career in journalism to concentrate on Christian writing, he said, "Just DO it."

Then there are moments like this after I cook for him, he showers me with appreciation like he is doing now. He has gotten up from his seat and scooped me up in his arms taking me into our boudoir, where the bed is undefiled.

As he makes love to me, possessively but tenderly, I can't stop the tears from flowing as I try to push his betrayal out of my eyes. He must feel them as he stops his ministrations and positions himself to look me in the eyes.

"Janine, sweetheart, why are you crying?" I decide to be upfront and honest.

"I love you so much, and I don't want to lose you to anyone else."

Episode Two
Seth

What did she just say? Can she possibly know my secret, my weakness, my shame? My mind tells me no way, but my heart and my gut know different. I stop worshiping her body with my hands and mouth and lift myself to look into her eyes. The brokenness I see sends a dagger to my heart. *She knows. How?*

"Sweetheart, why are you thinking of losing me?" I ask, hoping I am wrong, and she doesn't know about or suspect my infidelity. I gently wipe the tears away from her beautiful caramel face with the tips of my thumbs. She allows me to do it, so I lean in to kiss each of her cheeks.

"Seth, I know." She says in the softest whisper and I almost miss it. I stop again, but this time, my heart is beating so hard, I know she hears it.

"You know what, Janine?" *Dear Lord, let this be about something else. If you can do this for me, I promise I will live for you.* I think this prayer, knowing better that I can't make deals with God when my actions have caught

up with me. Janine is my everything. I don't know why I
have risked it all for someone that doesn't matter.

"I know where you were this afternoon. I know
where you were last Tuesday and all the Tuesdays before
that." She says that as more tears stream down. Guilt hits
me like I've never felt. My wife, my love, is telling me she
knows about my infidelity, in the sweetest way. I am an
evil man. I rise off of her and off the bed. I can no longer
look her in the eye. I put on the t-shirt I had previously
discarded when I thought this night would end differently. I
make my way over to the recliner in our bedroom and drop
down there. I then look up at her while she sits up in the
bed.

"Why Seth? Have I not been good to you? What
would make you need to go somewhere else?"

"Honey, I'm sorry. It means nothing. I won't see
her again." Even to myself, that sounds lame, but all other
words fail me.

Episode Three
Seth

"Seriously? That's your answer?" Janine looks at me with a raised eyebrow as she folds her arms over her breasts. She is waiting for a better answer; the only problem is I don't have one.

"Babe, I'm sorry. I just got caught up. It doesn't mean anything. I'll end it." I get up and walk toward the nightstand where my phone is on the charger. I will call Monica right now. She is not worth me losing my wife. I've always known that but couldn't stop seeing her. Now that my infidelity is exposed, it's over.

"What are you doing?" She asks me with a look of incredulity.

"I'm calling Monica to tell her it's over." I unplug my phone, scroll down my call list, and select the number for Monica. My wife looks on, and I'm feeling nervous about her calm demeanor.

Monica

I'm enjoying a nice hot shower, and the water is massaging my aching limbs. Seth always leaves me tired after our hook ups. I am thinking of all the ways we pleasured each other when I hear his ring tone, "Saving All My Love for You" by Whitney Houston. It's old school, but it rings true for my current situation. I don't shut the water off, not wanting to miss his call, and almost trip over myself opening my shower door. I get it open and scurry to my phone, sitting on the counter, while I'm dripping wet.

"Hi, there, handsome."

"Hi, Monica, I want to make you aware that I have placed our call on speaker, and my wife can hear us."

What the . . .? I'm not sure why I look at the phone, it's not as if he called me via video chat, but I look at it all the same.

"Monica, are you there?" I hear Seth call out.

"Yes, I am here, and what is the purpose of your call?" Maybe he needs me to cover for him—or us—so we can continue. That is the only reason I don't hang up in his face. He clears his throat before speaking.

"My wife is aware of our affair, and I am calling to let you know it's over." My breath catches in my throat, and I feel like he is ending my life, not just our affair. *Do I respond to this?* Can I form words to tell him this is not the end, I say how and when? That has been the nature of our affair for the past year and a half. I do what his wife can't or won't, and he caters to my needs. Surely, he is just saying this not to get kicked out of his house. But Seth doesn't have to worry about a place. He pays my rent; he can live here. I choose not to act irrationally. I don't hear his wife Janine saying a word, so I won't either.

I only say, "Okay, Seth."

I disconnect and get back in the shower that luckily is still hot. I will pretend like that conversation never happened.

Use this link to keep reading Seth and Janine's story – It Won't Prosper.

Made in the USA
Columbia, SC
18 May 2017